Amalee

❀ Amalee ❀

by Dar Williams

SCHOLASTIC PRESS · NEW YORK

Library of Congress Cataloging-in-Publication Data
Williams, Dar.
Amalee / Dar Williams.— 1st ed.
p. cm.
Summary: Amalee is being raised by her single father and his
group of eccentric friends, and when he becomes seriously ill
everyone pitches in to try to cope with the ensuing fear and chaos.
ISBN 0-439-39563-1 — ISBN 0-439-39564-X (pbk.)
[1. Friendship — Fiction.   2. Single-parent families — Fiction.
3. Sick — Fiction.]   I. Title.
PZ7.W6559245   Am   2004
[Fic] — dc22   2003020079

10 9 8 7 6 5 4 3 2 1   04 05 06 07 08

Printed in the U.S.A.   37
First edition, May 2004

typography by Steve Scott
book was set in Clarion

For Michael and the Robinson Family

Acknowledgments

I want to thank all the kids who have shown up at my concerts and said hello, with an extra thanks to Peter Swanson, Will Berger, Lillie Bea Scheer, Juliet Swanson, Tommy Farley, Jimmy Farley, and Joe Berger (and their parents), and to Louise and Marilyn MacDonald. Thanks also to my parents and to all my friends who remember what it's like to be eleven years old and who provided insights for this book, Nerissa Nields, Katryna Nields, Patty Romanoff, Melinda Adamz, Patty Smythe, Kate Bennis, Lisa Wittner, Lisa Seelinger, Curry Rose Mills-Hoskey, Anne Weiss, and, of course, my husband, Michael Robinson.

Constant thanks to my manager, Ron Fierstein, and to Lisa Arzt.

And most of all, thanks to my editor, David Levithan, who understands and believes in kids of every age (including mine), and who patiently helped me tell a better story than I thought I could. Thanks to Randi Reisfeld and everyone at Scholastic for their help, too, and to the security staff at the Cathedral Church of St. John the Divine in New York City for not kicking me out as I wrote in various empty chapels.

CHAPTER ONE

The Night I Opened My Big Mouth

Imagine six kids packed into a car, laughing and talking on their way to get pizza and root beer, planning to see a great movie afterward. Now imagine that five of those kids are actually forty-two years old, and they're still packed in that car, and the sixth passenger is eleven years old. That's me, Amalee Everly. The other five would be my dad and his four big, goofy friends.

And there I was, on a freezing night in early March, going to the movies with them.

They'd all gone to college together, and then they had vowed to continue having fun together, to hang out together, and to be there for each other forever, till death do they part. I don't know what they would have done if they'd all had kids, but only one of them did. That, of course, was my dad, David, who was driving and smiling as each of them squoze in.

First stop was his oldest friend, Phyllis. He'd known her since he was six. Phyllis was tall and had a big smile that made me think of all the pictures of her and my dad from when they were kids. She would slide into the front seat and immediately swivel around to ask me about whatever I was studying, or drill me on a new word, which, I have to admit, I always liked. I loved new words. Tonight's word was illuminate, or "ih-LOOM-in-ate, ih-LOOOOOM-in-ate," as Phyllis pronounced it, widening her large brown eyes. It means to shed light on something, like a floodlight *illuminates* the street "or, if a person wants more information, she can say, 'illuminate me.' The same way she could say 'enlighten me.' They both mean 'show me the light.'"

So a person can be illuminated, too.

Carolyn jumped in next. "You're lucky I called the movie theater ahead of time," she announced as she got in the backseat. "I had to reserve tickets, it was so popular. I *told you* this town needed more foreign films." I groaned quietly. That was Carolyn — unsmiling, with her short red hair sticking out in all directions. She always had a lot of energy, but not cheerful energy. She was very serious, especially about her favorite topic (herself) and she was a painter who often expressed disgust for a world that didn't care about art (especially her art).

We got to Joyce's house next, and, true to her nature, she hopped in beside me, black hair bouncing, a bright scarf spilling all over her coat. She moved into the car, gave me a hug that said, "I know you don't like to be hugged. This will be short," squeezed Phyllis and my dad on the shoulder, and nodded to Carolyn, who practically had a DON'T TOUCH ME sign around her neck. Joyce was always looking out for people's feelings, because she was a therapist. After her round of hellos, Joyce quietly started straightening and retying her scarf, smiling and humming to herself.

Finally, John opened the door, and it was time for me to ride on someone's lap. He was mostly bald, very twinkly — this was the best description for his eyes and the way he laughed — and altogether pretty hefty.

It was crowded, it was pretty boring, and the worst thing was that we did this every single week. Every Friday I sat on a different lap, and a different person would complain about his or her life — except for my dad, who always drove and never complained.

This week I was on Joyce's lap. Her lap was actually the best one, because she would always sneak me breath mints. Her minty breath was the best in the car.

Tonight, as it turned out, it was John's turn to complain. He was the headwaiter at a fancy restaurant, but he wanted to be a chef.

"I swear I almost quit my job last night!" he said in his broad Georgia accent. He was always saying he was going to quit his job. But he never did.

"Really?" My dad sounded surprised, even though we'd already heard this on plenty of Fridays.

John wanted to have his own restaurant. So how far had he come in making his dream come true? Well, he was good at giving detailed reports about how awful his job was. "Oh, David!" he moaned, "the chef doesn't know how to cook! Customers keep sending their dinners back to the kitchen. Too cold, too soggy, *burnt*. And you know what else? Even when he gets it right, his food is plain. Just plain food that people could have made at home. Going to a restaurant should be special. People go there for birthdays and anniversaries. They need *special* food! They need *exciting* food! I left a wonderful linzer torte recipe for him, you know, with a few tips, just to get him excited about cooking again. He's such a mean-spirited, depressed, lazy cow! Do you know what he did?"

Phyllis chimed in. She had a terrible problem with talking. And talking, and talking. "John found the recipe folded up at his headwaiter station," she said now. "No comment and no thanks."

"So you know what I'm going to do?" John asked. Then he answered himself. "I'm going to march into that bank on Monday, get a loan, and start *my own* restaurant. And the first dessert on the menu will be *my own* linzer torte."

"Oh, John, that's a very healthy way to deal with your disappointment!" said Joyce. Being a therapist, she loved it when people said nice things about themselves or made big, bold plans for their future. She was very popular in this car on Fridays. "Using your anger as rocket fuel to start your own project. That is a great use of energy."

Joyce had almost a little girl's voice. Phyllis liked to call her "tenderhearted." She cried whenever she saw something sad, beautiful, happy, or related to the autumn. "Oh, the fall!" she would say in her slightly munchkin voice. "Yellow leaves, yellow school buses! Kids walking to school." And then we'd see the tears, and Phyllis would pull a tissue from the bottomless pocket of her sweater and talk a little too long about anything that would help Joyce quiet down. Joyce thought she was a bad therapist because she cried so much. She learned to get two boxes of tissues — one for her clients, one for herself.

John was very happy to hear Joyce's opinion.

"That's right, Joyce," he said. "My anger gives me energy! Henri's unworthiness as a chef is the last straw!"

I couldn't stand it. I felt so cramped, so annoyed, and so sick of the same conversation every Friday.

"You always say it's the last straw, John," I pointed out.

I felt Joyce's legs stiffen beneath me, even as she wiped her nose.

Phyllis said, "What do you mean, Amalee?"

I let it all out. "I mean that every week is the last straw! Every week we pretend that John is really going to start a restaurant."

"And I'm sure he will, Amalee," Joyce gasped.

"And I'm sure he *won't*," I answered. I didn't mean to say it. I meant to say that John should just do what he said he was going to do. But instead, I felt like I'd just put a curse on him.

The silence that followed made it hard to breathe.

Carolyn spoke up from where she was wedged against the window. "Wow. That was mean." As always, Carolyn didn't hesitate to tell us what she thought.

The car was silent again. Joyce sucked on her mint nervously. In her little bird voice she said, "Well, really . . ." But nothing after that.

"Amalee's right," said John sadly. "I'm always saying

I'm going to do something, and then I don't. I'm unmotivated. *I'm* the lazy cow."

"You are not!" Phyllis protested.

"John, you work harder than anyone I know," said my dad.

I couldn't say a thing. I had no idea I could say something that would hurt a person so much. John sounded like a different person, as if he'd taken off a bright mask to show that he was just some really depressed guy underneath. I liked John. I'd always liked him. He annoyed me, too, but he'd always made it clear he would move a mountain for me if he had to. Now suddenly everyone was jumping in to defend him against what I'd just said.

Phyllis sprang into action. She was the big problem solver in the office at my school, where she worked. Now she was going to solve the big problem in this small car. "John," she said, "what you need is a plan. You don't have to go and get a loan right away. You need to plan this out, step by step, put it all on a list and follow the list. Then you'll have a restaurant and everyone will be happy. You know why? Because you are a better chef than Henri. You have more imagination. Your food is more special."

"A plan," John said, moping. "If I gave you all the plans I'd written over the last ten years, you'd have a lifetime supply of toilet paper."

"Oh, John!" cried Joyce.

"Do you need a tissue, Joyce?" asked Phyllis.

"Yes, thank you. Sorry."

We got to the pizza place. The car stopped. Everyone sat for a moment before we got out. No more laughing. No more dreams and schemes, just a bunch of tired people at the end of a long, disappointing week. You didn't have to be an adult to know what that felt like. The only sound was four doors opening and four doors shutting.

So this Friday was different from other Fridays. Because I, the only real kid in the car, opened my big mouth and ruined it.

❖ CHAPTER TWO ❖

This on Top of Everything Else

The movie, to make things worse, was in Swedish. We all squinted to read the subtitles. My dad left the theater a couple of times. "Where's he going?" I asked Carolyn. She was always good for a straight answer. (Unless it involved her paintings.)

"I think he's having those headaches again," she whispered. He'd had some bad headaches, but I didn't know they were so bad he'd leave a movie so often. Then I realized I'd probably made them worse.

Since Carolyn hadn't said "Shhhhh," I also asked, "By the way, who's that guy in the movie playing chess on the beach?"

"That's Death," she said. Spooky.

I looked over at John. He was tapping his foot, not even watching the movie. Lost in his own lost thoughts.

I felt awful all over again.

The movie was long and depressing. Even Phyllis muttered to Joyce afterward that it was "endless."

The trip home felt that way, too.

My dad spoke up after he'd dropped everyone off, waiting as they trudged through the snowbanks and up to their front doors. "Honey," he said, "John is frustrated that he hasn't opened up his restaurant."

"I know," I told him.

"So what I'm trying to say is, you don't need to point it out to him," he continued quietly. "You didn't do anything wrong. I know he sounds like a broken record, but we've got to let him do this in his own time."

"I know."

"I'm not mad, though."

"Whatever," I said, and looked out the window. He wasn't mad? I hadn't done anything wrong? What was he thinking? I had behaved terribly. Maybe this was his way of giving up on me. Trying to make me better had tired him out and now, with this headache, he was done. He didn't think I could behave any better than this.

I saw my reflection in the window. Short brown hair just a little bit longer than a boy's, which is what I asked for. Carolyn always insisted on cutting my hair, and she would always end by saying, "It didn't turn out the way I wanted it to, but it doesn't look horrible." For all I knew, it looked ridiculous. I looked at my little blue eyes and little mouth. I'd always liked my eyes, because when I was about eight, I realized that I could make them look unusually serious. But when I smiled, I looked like a very friendly person.

Not that I'd smiled a lot this year, or that I'd been friendly.

I added tonight's disaster to the pile of things that weren't going right in my life. I hated school. I didn't have one thing to look forward to. Not a single human being. I didn't mind what we were studying, even, but I was in middle school now, which meant less colors, less friendliness, and more meanness. And there was another problem. I was meaner, too. Or I felt meaner.

I thought of the time a couple weeks before winter vacation when Ellen Walken, on her eleventh birthday, was talking with me and Hally Masters about going skiing. She had told me she was going to ski on a difficult slope, something with the word "diamond" in it. Frances Perry, a nice kid who never said a bad word to anyone, and who seemed a little lonely, suddenly jumped into the conversation. We were in the cafeteria. "Me, too!" she said. "We go skiing, and my ski class is going to go on that slope this year!"

All she was saying was *I have something in common with you, or someone, or anyone.* Nothing else.

Ellen looked insulted that Frances had cut into our conversation. "What state do you ski in?" she asked slowly.

"What state?" Frances asked, frowning.

"What state — of the *United* States — do you ski in?" Ellen repeated, as if each word were its own sentence.

"Oh, uh, the state of New York," Frances almost whispered, as if this were a trick question. And it was, in a way.

"State of New York, as in Catskill Mountains, where the black-diamond course is basically a big hill?" Ellen accused.

"Yeah, it's the Catskill Mountains. Where is your ski place?" Frances asked.

"Utah. Rocky Mountains," Ellen said, pronouncing it "YOU-taw, RRROCK-y mountains."

That's when I should have stopped being friends with her. That's when I should have said, "So basically, you ski far away enough that no one can tell if you're lying." But I only came up with that while I was brushing my teeth that night. At the time, I did something worse. I felt myself nodding my head, as if to comment that the Rocky Mountains were, in fact, definitely bigger.

Frances looked burned, because she was. I had stood

by and watched, and I'd gone along with Ellen. She was so hard to please. But I always felt like I was only one step away from winning her over completely. Making her like me. And making Hally like me, too.

In fifth grade, I had lots of friends. Now, in sixth grade, they all ended up in other classrooms, and I had two new friends maybe, Ellen and Hally. We were seated together at the beginning of school, and for some reason they liked me.

They were smarter than the other kids, or they acted that way. Ellen would ask me questions about the news. Did I know the name of the president? The vice president?

I wanted to impress them, so I asked Phyllis about the government. She knew everything and tried to fit in a complete explanation over one dinner at our house. This was one time when I didn't mind her talking and talking.

When I went to school the next day, I knew all the answers to what Ellen had asked, plus all the other information Phyllis had packed into my head. I guess I was showing off when I asked, "Do you know who the Secretary of the Interior is? And what her job is?"

Ellen didn't answer, saying, "Everybody knows that. How many Senators are there?"

That's when I realized that Ellen liked smart people,

but not *too* smart. So I said, "One hundred or fifty. I can't remember."

"It's a hundred." She rolled her eyes. "Two for every state."

I think Hally was the smartest of us. She had the nicest clothes and a soft voice. Whenever she spoke, she said something very interesting. I admired Hally, and I found myself wanting to impress her.

Ellen made fun of everyone, while Hally would say one thing every once in a while, like, "Alex shouldn't wear those pants with that sweater. She has often been a careless dresser." She used the English language in a strange way. With her blond hair around her face, I couldn't help thinking of her as a little intelligent fairy, not quite from the human world.

All the teachers liked Ellen and Hally. I thought these two girls were good for me. They made me think more and learn about things like the government. They told me when my clothes matched.

The only problem was, none of the other kids wanted to be around us.

Actually, I guess *we* didn't want to be around *them,* either.

One girl was particularly annoying: Lenore Nielson. I

had been friends with her since third grade, but I never liked her. She was bossy and basically just loud. She used to explain that I had to be her friend. Once you were a friend, she said, you had to stay loyal, even if you didn't like your friend at all. I felt like she was threatening me, but when she'd invited me to movie after movie, sleepover after sleepover, I always said yes. What if she was right? I never wanted to be a bad friend, even to a mean friend like Lenore.

But then things changed. When I started being friends with Ellen and Hally, I discovered that I could turn my back on Lenore just like they did, and Lenore would actually go away. I never had to say anything mean. I could just say nothing. It was such a relief! After years of hearing her boast about her grades, whine about her younger brothers, and create complicated games where I had to follow everything she said, she was gone.

So that was my life. Ellen, Hally, and I were envied and — I realized more and more — feared. People watched us out of the corners of their eyes, and walked by quickly.

By October, I could see that I was really changing. My brain felt sharper. I put my clothes out the night before school, and I made sure I had what I needed for class. I tried not to let any old stupid thing come out of my mouth. I tried to be more like Hally. Ellen talked a lot, but she was clever.

I actually liked everything we were learning about, especially new words and history. I felt like I could be smart around them, and we could challenge each other. Phyllis called this kind of thing "sharpening your wits" and said it was why she liked hanging out with Mr. Spiro, the librarian.

The strange thing was, the teachers liked Ellen and Hally, but they didn't seem to like me as much.

I mean, our music teacher, Ms. Bernstein, was a hippie, so she liked everyone. Mrs. Donaldson, the math teacher, didn't really like anyone. Mr. Hankel, the science teacher, called me a "swell kid" once. But there was also Ms. Severance, the English and social studies teacher. I thought she was brilliant, but she liked Hally and Ellen much better than me, which didn't seem fair.

Once Hally turned to Ellen and said, "She should wear bigger earrings, to compensate for her long face."

Ellen said, "And she also wears that sweater, like, every day. I hope she washes it!"

Ms. Severance wore that sweater a couple of times a week. I knew because I loved it. It was a soft mossy green with buttons that looked like shells. And she wore little earrings that sparkled when she turned toward the window. There was nothing wrong with that. I didn't notice her long face until Hally pointed it out.

I said nothing, and that's when I knew I was like the other kids, too afraid to speak up.

Finally, the day before winter vacation, I saw a note that Hally wrote to Ellen. It said, "She could use a professional haircut: a salon." There was an arrow underneath the words. I closed my eyes and figured out that, yes, the arrow had been pointed at me.

So I felt uncomfortable around my friends for a good reason. They made fun of me, too. Under Hally's writing, Ellen wrote, "Is she a boy or girl???"

I showed the note to Ellen and she said, "You took a piece of paper off the dirty floor, uncrumpled it, and read a personal note between me and Hally? It wasn't about you. And it was PRIVATE."

From then on, when she and Hally passed notes, they wrote PRIVATE on them in big letters. There were no more sleepovers, and no more laughing together.

On a good day, I said one thing that made them smile.

After vacation, I asked Frances if she'd had a good time skiing, but by this time she expected the trick question she'd gotten from Ellen. She said, "What do you care?" I couldn't blame her, but it made me feel like walking poison when it came to friends.

* * *

My dad's friends, on the other hand, all wanted to be my friends, but that was because they loved my dad. Why was I so bad at making my own friends?

Dad always said he was lucky to have the friends he did. He talked about how they helped him be a single dad and how they convinced him to keep me when he wasn't so sure he should.

When my dad was in his twenties, he lived with his girlfriend, my mother, because of me, their daughter. The story goes that they met at a restaurant where they worked. Then they had me. They got different shifts, hers at night and his during the day. They hardly saw each other, but they didn't have to get baby-sitters.

My mother, Sally, was unhappy. I knew this because Carolyn once said, "We all know Sal had that baby to make her parents angry."

Lovely. My mom had me as revenge.

My dad and his other friends all jumped in and said, "Noooo, noooo, she loved you sooooo much."

But if my mom was unhappy, the next part of the story made more sense.

One day she said, "I thought I could do this, but I can't."

"This" was me. She couldn't handle it. Me. And so she left.

Dad met with his friends. "This kid deserves a stable environment," he said, and they said, "Yes!"

And he said, "So I should put her up for adoption," and his friends said, "No!"

They told my dad that he could raise me, because they would help. Apparently, it ended with John saying, "David, this will be an adventure!"

Well, I liked that story, because I liked the ending. I loved my dad. He was nice to everyone, including me. He taught philosophy at the State University of New York, New Paltz, or SUNY New Paltz, and he would have students over for holiday parties in December. They liked my dad, too.

He and I always spoke sympathetically about my mother, as if she were a friend who had never figured out what she wanted. She died in a car accident soon after she left. Poor Sally. I really did feel sorry for her.

I looked over now at my dad driving and wanted to get back into a conversation. I was sick of feeling so quiet and frowning all the time. I asked about his headache.

"It's not good," Dad admitted. "It's in the back of my head and neck."

"I know those," I said. "It feels like a robot has you in its pincer?"

Dad laughed. "That's exactly what kind of headache it is."

And that's what a great dad he was. I knew he had to be mad at me for what I'd said to John, but he still laughed. And unlike Ellen or Hally or Lenore, he never called me "crazy." None of his friends did, either. Of course, that's because they were all pretty crazy themselves.

But they had helped raise me. In some ways, I'd grown up with five parents. Sometimes I thought I had only one, but he was a very, very good one.

CHAPTER THREE

Phyllis Looks for an Easy Way to Say a Hard Thing and Almost Succeeds

I was getting ready for school the Monday after the movie weekend, after I'd opened my mouth. I hadn't laid out my clothes. Suddenly, I didn't like any of my clothes. I thought of Hally quietly noticing the pills on my sweater or the little ink stain on my pants.

I heard my dad getting ready for work. He taught two classes at the college on Mondays.

On my way to the kitchen, I was surprised to see Phyllis's car in the driveway. My mind filled with that terrible silence in the car after I'd dropped that bomb, telling John to give it up.

Phyllis was polite. She didn't seem mad, but I couldn't tell. She didn't talk and talk and talk like she usually did. She was a little spacey as she drank her coffee and I poured some cereal. I tried to make small talk as if I were going to work like her and my dad.

"Another day, another dollar," I said, shaking my head.

"Would you like a ride to school?" Phyllis asked. "I'm not going to work today, actually, but I can drop you off."

"Why aren't you going?"

"I'm driving your dad to the doctor," she answered casually.

"Which doctor?" I asked.

Phyllis crossed and re-crossed her long legs. "He hasn't been feeling well."

"What do you mean? You mean the headaches?"

"Yeah, and he's been feeling dizzy. A little dizzy."

"Is that bad?" I was worried now.

"It's something to pay attention to." Phyllis was looking into the next room, hoping my dad would come in and finish the explanation.

"How bad is that? I mean, how dizzy is he?"

"He fainted."

"When?"

"Yesterday. You were at the library. Don't get me wrong, people faint sometimes. We're just being careful. So we're both calling in sick today. Don't tell anyone I'm just the driver." She stopped herself from going on, and she smiled.

"So this is just to make sure he's okay?" I asked, still nervous.

"Exactly. And you know how careful I like to be." She was right about that. "I said, 'Nuh-uh, no driving for you until you see a doctor.' If he fainted in the car — I can't even think of it. So I'm cutting school."

I knew it had to be a big deal if Phyllis was cutting school. "I'll tell them you've got a huge rash with blisters," I promised her.

"Thank you," she said with a near smile. "Then they won't miss me."

"Well, hello," my dad said as he came in for breakfast. "Are we taking you to school today?"

"Yeah, and then you're going to the doctor," I said. I looked at him closely, to see if I could notice something really wrong. Mostly he looked like he hadn't slept at all.

Dad looked at Phyllis. "Yup," he said, "I'm sure I'm fine. It's part of being healthy to be careful."

Sure. I narrowed my eyes to look very serious, but they didn't notice.

Dad insisted on sitting in the backseat of the car, and I got a little chill down my spine. Sitting in the front seat, I felt like I was the parent and we were dropping my dad off at school. But when the car stopped, it was me jumping out and going up the steps of the middle school.

I walked in past Hally and Ellen on the way to my new seat. The seating had changed, and that was fine with me. Ellen was talking with Lenore. "New York was founded by the Dutch," she said. "They had a boat called the *Half Moon*. The *Mayflower* went to Massachusetts, not the Hudson River." And then she added what she always added: "Everybody knows that."

I groaned and quickly passed both of them.

How was I going to make it through this day? I don't even know if I did. I could only think about Dad at the doctor's.

At lunch, I went to my hiding place, the side of the stage we had in the gym. Once, during an assembly, I looked into the dark wings of the stage and knew I could go there to be alone. Sure enough, the door to the backstage was always open, even though it had the word "PRIVATE" in chipped letters. There was never anyone there. Today I went backstage and felt so lonely that I tried to read a book in the dark.

The teachers' moods matched the weather, gloomy and heavy. Ms. Severance didn't wear my favorite sweater. She hardly looked at us, either.

After school, I walked home through the snow. I knew a shortcut through the woods, and that's the way I liked to go.

Phyllis's car was in the driveway again, and so was Carolyn's. I didn't feel good about this.

"Hi, Amalee," Joyce said in her squeaky, teary voice as I walked in. She was there with Carolyn and Phyllis, who had their heads bowed.

"Hi," I said. "How did it go? Where's Dad?"

They made Joyce explain, because she was the therapist. My dad was in the hospital, and would be for a few days.

"What???" I exploded.

Phyllis jumped in, "Now, the doctor is being careful —"

"A few days?" I repeated. "That's not *careful,* that's *worried.*"

Phyllis and Joyce started talking at once. Words of comfort, words of hope to cover up words of fear and words of despair. My dad called these words *euphemisms.* "Stop it with all of those words you use!" I shouted. Joyce covered her mouth and Phyllis turned away. I froze up and couldn't apologize, but I wanted to. They were just trying to help, I knew.

Luckily Carolyn spoke up. "All right, all right, you can see it, Amalee. We're all a little worried. But actually the doctor said not to be worried."

Okay, that was better. If we were all scared, then I wasn't the only one in the dark. We all were.

Phyllis said, "I'm going to stay with you."

And she did. She stayed after Joyce and Carolyn left. It wasn't as weird as I thought it would be. She was like my dad's sister.

We ate spaghetti that night. After she convinced me that my dad was really fine and that there was only the slightest chance that something was wrong, I asked Phyllis why I didn't see other adults walking around with a pack of friends like my dad did. "Well, some people get married and kind of keep to themselves, and none of us are married, well not anymore," she thought out loud. "But you know what I think it is? Your dad is an only child, so he turns all his friends into brothers and sisters. I mean, I guess you do that, too."

"No, I don't," I said with emphasis. *Emphatically* — a word Ms. Severance had taught us.

"Is there, um, something wrong at school?" she asked slowly.

"What would be wrong?" I didn't want to talk about it.

"Do you have any friends?" she asked.

"Yes, they're just at school."

"I see," she said. She knew I was lying.

The phone rang and we both ran for it. It was Dad.

He said, "Hey, there! I hope I don't sound too funny.

They have to knock me out to do these tests. Do I sound like I'm talking through a tube?"

"No!" I laughed. He sounded fine. After I got off the phone, I excused myself quickly from the table and went to my room. And cried and cried.

Phyllis stayed for three more days. We had spaghetti for three more nights. That was a nice thing about her. She didn't care if we had the same thing three nights in a row.

She didn't ask any more questions about school or friends. We watched the news together, and she tried to explain what was going on in the government. It was an interesting change in my life, but I was looking forward to being with my dad again.

On Friday afternoon, Phyllis and Joyce were pulling out of my driveway as I got home from school.

"We're going to get your dad!" Phyllis said cheerfully.

"Let me come," I said.

"Uh, you don't want to go all the way to Westchester," Phyllis said, wrinkling her nose in sympathy.

"Sure I do," I told her.

Phyllis looked really nervous and sighed. "Okey-dokey, then."

"So," Joyce chattered as we drove down the highway, "what are you up to in school?"

"We're building a rocket."

"Really?"

"Yeah. It's just a one-person rocket. We're sending Mr. Hankel up. It's kind of a combination science project and retirement party."

Phyllis snorted. I'd made a joke to see how serious things were. If we were all laughing, everything had to be okay. Right?

Not right. As soon as we pulled into the hospital parking lot, I knew something was wrong.

"Do you have a book you can read?" Joyce asked. "You know, so you can stay in the car?"

"Why can't I come up?" I asked. I was more than ready to see my dad.

Phyllis came clean. "He's really out of it, Honey. He's feeling very sick."

I could tell Joyce was getting teary-eyed.

"It turns out he has something like the flu, but it's in his spine," Phyllis went on. "Which means he needs medication, and sleep, and . . . and time."

"Please," Joyce pleaded, "stay in the car for now. We'll bring him out."

And so I stayed, obedient as a golden retriever who sticks his nose out the window that's rolled down about an inch. They disappeared for about ten minutes. A flu in his spine. I thought of Mr. Hankel's diagram of the spinal cord.

Mr. Hankel always wanted to prove that every organ had an essential function (except, of course, the appendix). But he was more serious about a few things, like the heart, the brain, the spine, and the spinal fluid inside the spine. Mr. Hankel called the spinal fluid "the stuff of life" because it was also the brain fluid, or "the brain bath," he called it. He showed us how the fluid helped the spine act like a flexible tube that allowed us to bend and curve our backs. He made us bend and curve our backs and think about how flexible we were. He was a good teacher, I suddenly thought. That's when I realized I was so scared, I just wanted someone as big and slow and unmysterious as Mr. Hankel to come and quietly explain everything to me.

Then I saw my dad. They brought him out in a wheelchair looking half asleep.

"Hi, Dad!" I called, jumping out of the car, hoping I could cheer him up. But he looked confused.

"What are you doing here?" he asked.

"We're here to bring you home," Phyllis said.

Joyce was walking with the doctor, Dr. Nurstrom, who was tall and gloomy looking. "He'll need to come back and see me tomorrow and the next day and probably three times a week, at least," he was saying, coldly nodding to my dad. Phyllis and Joyce looked panicked.

Suddenly, Joyce seemed extremely warm and friendly. "Dr. Nurstrom, I have a very unusual idea," she said. "I know we aren't living in the Wild West here, but I have a picture in my mind of an old-fashioned doctor making a house call."

"No," said Dr. Nurstrom. "I need to see him."

"You don't know someone you trust around Rosendale? Someone who could stop in?"

"Rosendale?" He frowned. "I live in Woodstock."

"We're right on your way to work, then," Joyce pointed out. I noticed how pretty she was looking at this moment, with flushed cheeks that almost matched the red in her scarf.

"Dr. Nurstrom, we will cook you breakfast, make you lunch, make you coffee," Phyllis begged. "This drive would be so difficult for him. Imagine what it's like for him to be driven around in my car, with all the dog hair and the mess." I was always surprised to catch an adult in a big fat lie.

Phyllis didn't have a dog.

"I make good coffee," Joyce added.

At that moment, my dad lifted his head to protest. He couldn't even do that.

I reached out my hand and said, "Hush." I tried not to cry. I looked up and saw that everyone was looking at me.

"I, uh, think there are some rail trails around Rosendale where I could go running in the mornings," Dr. Nurstrom said reluctantly.

"Yes, there certainly are," Joyce agreed.

Dr. Nurstrom looked very worried, but then he smiled the best he could and said, "Yes, I can do this."

Then Joyce started to cry. I almost groaned. She put her head on Phyllis's shoulder and bawled.

Dr. Nurstrom put his hand on her back. "Of course, I can do this."

As Joyce was helping my dad into the car, Dr. Nurstrom asked if Joyce was my dad's girlfriend. I shuddered at the thought.

Phyllis said, "No, she's just a good friend. We're all good friends."

"He's lucky," said Dr. Nurstrom, and I remembered that not all people have friends like my dad's.

✿ CHAPTER FOUR ✿

The Chaos Begins

That night, our house had all the comforts of a bus station. Dad's friends tracked mud into the house, making a path from the front door to his room, bringing in pillows, moving Dad's stereo by his bed, and leaving their fast-food bags all over the place.

Dad slept through most of this, once waking up and saying, "I'm fine. I'm awake," as if he'd fallen asleep in a class.

John was not there. Joyce, Carolyn, and Phyllis brushed past one another. I noticed that they had less and less to do. I retreated to my room. I knew they were about to get to my name on their checklist of "things to take care of."

I could take care of myself, but that didn't matter. They would find me.

Sure enough, I heard a knock on my door while I was playing solitaire on my computer. It was Joyce.

Soft knock, soft voice. "Can I come in?" she asked, coming in. I just wanted her soft therapist voice to go away!

"Hi," she said. I was silent. And I was losing the game, which didn't help.

"Solitaire on a computer!" she exclaimed with a laugh. "Wow, you kids know so much about computers!"

It wasn't much different from a grandmother saying, "You kids and that television!"

But that doesn't mean I should have said what I said, which was, "You sound like a grandmother."

Whenever I saw Joyce looking in the mirror, she was sucking in her stomach and pushing up on her cheeks like they'd fallen off a shelf and she had to put them back. Over and over again.

Joyce took her hand off my shoulder.

I tried to think of something nicer to say, but I was so angry that she wasn't getting to the point, the point being that my dad was sick and she wanted to talk about it. I got mad that she was the therapist, but she couldn't think of the right words to say. So the next thing I said wasn't much better. "You do know how to use a computer, don't you?"

"Yes, actually, I do. I know how to use one very well." She didn't sound angry. She said, "You know, I can't imagine why I came up here to make you feel better when I feel so sad."

I was silent, still, but I wished I could say something like, "That's more like it."

But then she blew it again, sort of. She said, "Whenever I see solitaire, it reminds me of a song by Janis Ian."

Don't sing. Don't sing. Don't sing. She sang.

The song had something to do with the kind of girls who don't get asked to the prom, who stay home and play solitaire instead. I wanted to say, "Is that about you?" But I didn't. Even I knew that was too mean. Joyce wanted a boyfriend pretty badly. And I always caught her reading articles about having babies after forty, even though she had just turned forty last month.

I said, "Nice song." I was starting to win the game, which I hadn't stopped playing through the whole conversation. Was that who I was? A girl who's mean when she's losing and, well, keeps her mouth shut when she's winning? Still, I started to relax as I heard Joyce leaving the room, and saw I had won the game. For a short time, and for the first time all day, I felt only one thing, and that was relief.

✿ CHAPTER FIVE ✿

Donuts for the Doctor

I woke to absolute silence. Dad wasn't up yet. Then I remembered yesterday at the hospital. Was he okay? I stumbled out of bed and into the hall. His door was closed.

"Dad?" I called softly through the door. I heard nothing. "Dad?" I called again. Someone tapped me on the shoulder, and I shouted the only word I had in my mind, "DAD!"

I reeled around to Phyllis as she said, "Shhhh!! What's wrong?"

"Is he okay in there?" I asked.

"He's fine. He just needs to sleep."

"How do you know?" I challenged her.

Phyllis was stretching her arms. I realized she'd slept on the couch. Now she stopped and stared me down.

"I'm sorry," I apologized.

"It's okay," she said. "I understand. The doctor will be here in fifteen minutes. Otherwise I'd open the door and check. Let's get some breakfast. You got me all worried now, . . ." she muttered as she led me to the kitchen. "I bet Dr. Nurstrom likes strong coffee," she told herself as she measured the grounds.

"Uh, hello?" We heard a voice at the door. Dr. Nurstrom found his way to the kitchen. "Good morning." He looked big in our house. Not big like a bear. More like a giraffe.

"How do you like your coffee?" Phyllis asked.

"Oh, coffee, uh, yes. I'll have a small cup."

Phyllis pretended he'd answered the question.

"Are you going to check him now?" I asked. "We tried to check him but there was no sound."

"Why did you do that?" Dr. Nurstrom asked, suddenly frowning in my direction.

"I was worried," I said, terrified that I'd done something wrong.

"You shouldn't bother him," he said, heading out of the kitchen. Had I harmed my dad by calling out for him? Interrupted his sleep?

Dr. Nurstrom bumped into Phyllis, who stood in the doorway.

"I think it's pretty natural for Amalee to worry about her dad, don't you?" she asked as kindly as she could. "Here's your coffee."

"Oh, I, uh, yes, thank you. Um, worry, yes. People worry, of course." He turned back to look at me, then hurried down the hall.

Before I could thank Phyllis for sticking up for me, we heard someone else.

"Knock, knock," Joyce sang in her little voice.

"What's Joyce doing here? It's not her shift," Phyllis wondered out loud. *Aha.* So they *were* going to come in shifts. They all pretended to be relaxed about the situation, but they weren't planning on leaving me alone with Dad. I felt annoyed, but then I remembered how scared I'd felt when I couldn't hear any sound coming from his room.

Joyce burst into the room, weighed down under two grocery bags.

"Well, I got donuts for the doctor, but then I thought he might be into, you know, health food, so I got a few whole-grain bagels, and a mango, and orange juice, and some eggs in case he wants a couple." She caught herself rambling. "We want him to like it here," she explained. "This is really for David. David is worth finding out what the doctor likes for breakfast."

The three of us tiptoed down the hall and peeked in at Dr. Nurstrom and Dad, who looked a little better than he had yesterday.

Dr. Nurstrom was showing Dad how to use a bunch of things.

"Press this button to reach me immediately," he said, demonstrating on a box next to my dad's bed. "Or press this button to call an ambulance, and this button to call your daughter."

My back stiffened. Me?

"Ama doesn't have to do anything," Dad protested. He sounded almost too tired to speak. I felt bad that he was wasting his words on me.

"I can do things," I spoke up.

"You might need her if you fall or if you can't breathe," Dr. Nurstrom said coldly, as he turned on another machine. Couldn't breathe? What would I do about that?

Joyce stepped forward and said, "Dr. Nurstrom, this is a sensitive situation. I think we all feel a little nervous about this."

"Well, you'll have to deal with it," the doctor shot back.

I expected Joyce to melt into tears, but she didn't. "Dr. Nurstrom! We are doing the best we can, and that is very well. We're going to have questions and fears and *you're* going to have to deal with *that!*" she exclaimed. Dr. Nurstrom looked at all of us one by one. He seemed a little less stern, maybe even embarrassed. "Now," Joyce continued, more gently, "I have donuts, bagels, a mango, and orange juice for you. And eggs. What can I get you?"

We waited for Dr. Nurstrom to storm out of the room, but instead he spun around and faced Joyce. "You got all that food for me?"

Now Joyce looked embarrassed, and said, "Well, we're very grateful that you're here."

Dr. Nurstrom asked for a cinnamon donut, a mango, and a plain bagel.

"And . . . thank you," he added.

And that was that.

CHAPTER SIX

Okay, So John Really *Is* a Chef

Phyllis drove me to school on Monday, listing all the things she was going to do to make my life easier. First off, she was going to tell all my teachers about my dad.

"No, you can't," I said.

"Heavens! Why not?" she asked.

I had lots of reasons. What if everyone got worried about me and followed me around? I couldn't eat backstage anymore. And they probably wouldn't let me walk home.

I thought of Ms. Severance disliking me even more. She would think I was trying to get out of doing homework. And what if one of the teachers made an announcement to the class, telling the other kids about my dad? This was *my* business.

And then there was the guiltiest secret I had. I was

seen as a mean kid now. I had stood by while Ellen was mean to other kids. I had been silent, because I felt shy this year. I felt sad. I missed the paintings by the first graders that they used to put up in the hallways. I missed watching the third graders at recess. So I was quiet, and I let other kids think *they* had a problem, not me. Maybe if the kids knew my dad was sick, they would be mean back to me, as if they had been waiting for the right moment to attack.

"This has to be our secret," I insisted. "Do you promise?"

Phyllis said yes, but I could tell she felt very uncomfortable.

Lenore appeared out of nowhere as I was walking up the steps to school. "I wish someone drove *me* to school every morning," she panted, catching up with me. She didn't say it nicely.

"Hi, Lenore," I said. Dealing with Lenore was always so awful, especially today, when I was too worried to follow all my strategies: *Avoid her if you can. If you can't avoid her, be on guard for something mean she's going to say. When she says something mean, don't explode or she'll make it worse.*

"I've been working on my report on the Pilgrims. What's yours about?' she asked. Before I could answer, she said, "Hey, slow down! We're not late."

I gave in. I slowed down.

"I'm doing a report on the first Thanksgiving," I said.

"Oh, you took the *easy* topic," she replied.

I took the first Thanksgiving because John always made Thanksgiving dinner at our house. And it was always my favorite time of year. "Let us give thanks," he would announce, "that those of us who have lost their parents can be together" — that was everyone except John — "and that my father and stepmother, safe and sound in Georgia, don't require a visit from their fat, bald, cantankerous son until Christmas. I am obviously needed here in the meantime." Then he would present a huge, elaborately stuffed turkey, followed by a different exotic pie for every guest, from ginger mincemeat to vodka key lime pie, after which all of us would fight for the remote control and space on the couch. John always won, and we would watch black-and-white movies on TV.

I stopped in my tracks as Lenore kept walking and talking. Would there be another Thanksgiving like that? Were things about to change? I lost my breath.

I wasn't sure if I'd make it through the day. I decided to pretend I was a river rock, letting the river of whatever hard words I heard today wash over me.

I caught up with Lenore, muttering, "Yes, I'm sure I took the easy assignment. Maybe I was just feeling lazy."

"Laziness can be a bad habit," Lenore lectured as we walked.

The river of Lenore.

When Ms. Severance didn't call on me, when Mr. Hankel lost his temper at us, when Hally and Ellen observed that my shoe was untied, I let it wash over me. This stuff wasn't important. I actually felt a little sorry for them all. Why did everyone waste so much time being unkind?

I came home to my dad sleeping, so I tiptoed past his room. I looked around but didn't find any of his friends.

"Amalee," I heard him call. I backed up, feeling a little nervous. We were going to have the big talk now? The one about how sick he was? He looked a little less terrible than he had this morning and certainly yesterday. He was still pale, but less green and less clammy.

"How was school?" he asked. "Do you have a lot of homework?"

"I've got some," I answered.

"Do it here," he offered, pointing to his desk. "On the big desk."

"Okay," I said, carefully taking off the books and, at his suggestion, piling up his papers.

I sat on a couple of couch cushions and spread my books across the massive desktop of dark wood. No wonder people bought big antiques like this. It made my homework seem more important.

I looked over at my dad, who was already reading a book.

So, no talk. We worked together for almost two hours, with him drifting off and shaking himself awake. He offered to quiz me on the pulmonary system. I asked him if he wanted a sandwich first.

"There's nothing else to eat," I complained. "Everyone brought food this weekend, but then they stayed and ate it!"

"A sandwich would be perfect, Honey," he assured me.

The silence of the afternoon was contagious. The whole house was silent as the darkness came on. I shuddered a little as I slid around the kitchen floor in my socks, making peanut butter and jelly sandwiches. Should I just ask him if he was scared, maybe tell him not to worry about me, something like that? Maybe I could walk in and call him by his first name, the way we called my mother "Sally." "*David? Is there something you'd like to talk about?*" I'd ask, making my eyes look very sincere. I spread Phyllis's stiff health-food store peanut butter on the soft white bread Joyce had bought. Had they asked Dad if he was scared? I could ask Phyllis. I got out Carolyn's homemade preserves and said a little prayer that they wouldn't kill us all. Then I went upstairs.

Dad was smiling at me as if nothing were wrong. "Where are those science questions?" he asked. We were just going over the names of lung diseases when we heard a big clatter downstairs.

We looked at each other in alarm. Then we heard someone swearing. It was John.

I hadn't seen him since I'd insulted him. He was coming up the stairs, and before I could react, his head was in the room. "Hey ho," he called, "I hear you're bedridden, David. Hi, Amalee." I couldn't figure out how he was really feeling. "Oh, dear! Don't tell me you're eating sandwiches after two o'clock in the afternoon! How would you like a big healthy dinner?" I wondered if he knew how sick Dad was, or if any of us did for that matter.

"I'm not sure I can finish this!" Dad said, holding up my sandwich. "But make something for Amalee."

"And I'll make a little something for you later, too. Sandwiches for dinner . . . really!" John scoffed, disappearing.

"Go with him," Dad whispered. "I'm sleepy anyway." I wasn't sure, but Dad looked at me and knew what was going on. "C'mon, Honey," he said. "John's not mad. Go hang out with him." I'd missed the chance to find out how my dad was feeling about being sick. For now, at least.

I paused, then gathered up my homework and dropped it off in my room. I wanted to close the door and be alone, but I went downstairs.

John was standing in the kitchen with a big lumpy sack by his side and about ten bags of groceries on the counters.

"I've come to help," he said, as if this were a secret we were keeping from my dad. "This is my shift. I was supposed to be here at three! Don't tell Phyllis."

"You really have this shift thing down to a science," I said.

John fished a piece of paper out of his pocket. It was a schedule of all the times that he, Phyllis, Joyce, and Carolyn would be staying at the house. This was the kind of thing Phyllis would do.

John started pulling pots and pans out of his bag. "What in creation have you been eating around here?" he asked.

"Well, uh, sandwiches."

"Like the ones you were just eating? Sandwiches on white bread, with peanut butter and Carolyn's creepy preserves? Like that?" John looked like he was going into a trance of horror at the thought of it. "You think your father's going to get better eating that?" Then he opened his eyes wider and said, "You all are going to need some good food." Maybe he wanted to be alone. Maybe I just wanted to leave him alone. As mean as I'd been, he was being so dramatic, it was making me feel annoyed again. I started to leave.

"Ama, Hon, I need your help."

I flared my nostrils and stared up at the ceiling, and then I turned around.

"I don't know if I brought enough stuff. But you have some things. Thank God I stocked you up before the New Year's party. I'll need some flour, baking powder, baking soda, sugar, cinnamon, and if you could go to the cellar and get me some red wine. That's for the cook." He winked.

I went downstairs and got the wine. Then I went to the pantry and got all the stuff he asked for. I don't think it took more than five minutes, but when I got back, everything was set up. The sack was folded on top of the refrigerator. John looked up and said, "Let's go." He cracked an egg.

It's hard to remember what happened next. I just followed his orders.

"I need two cups of flour and another two cups of sifted flour."

"Bring me a cup of milk, but measure it in another

measuring cup. We'll do all the wet stuff in one and dry stuff in another."

There was some broth simmering on the stove that made the house smell like we were getting ready for a big dinner party.

Suddenly, he had three bowls going at once and was asking me to do three things at once.

"Chop the celery." I chopped while he stirred.

"Stir this." I stirred the broth with the celery while he sautéed garlic.

He left me stirring and sautéing at once, while he crossed over to two bowls. I saw him through a slight haze of flour.

"Three tablespoons heavy cream," he commanded from another station in the room.

Something was different about him. It was as if he were playing a chef in a movie, very confident and know-ledgeable. He covered one bowl to let some dough rise, and he pulled out another. He was turning pink from the heat in the kitchen. There were pots on two burners, and the stove was preheated for whatever he was kneading and covering. He was also a little out of breath.

"We need lots of eggs. Seven."

I cracked and stirred and checked on the garlic. I saw

at least four cartons of eggs and wondered how much more we were going to do.

"A tablespoon of vanilla." He tasted whatever was in the bowl. "Throw in another splash." He tasted it again. "Oh, I'm good! Now a dash of cinnamon and a cup of that broth from the stove. Careful, though! We'll freeze this stuffing for a night we cook a turkey."

He almost danced around the pots on the stove, stirring and smelling whatever was bubbling here and crackling there. Then he went to a bowl and emptied the contents into two bread pans. "Vegetarian meat loaf. Make sure the oven's set for four hundred." Soon the smell of chicken soup was joined by the meat loaf, not to mention the garlic stuffing.

A puff of steam as big as a genie rose up from the sink, and then John was carrying over a huge bowl of pasta. I quickly cleared some counter space and stood by his side, pulling big noodles out of the strainer for lasagna.

"Wow. You're a natural," he said, turning down the burner on the soup behind him. "Oh, by the way, I got you some root beer." That was nice.

He pulled the risen dough out of one of the first bowls and plopped it on a rolling board. Then he took some dough and rolled it out with a rolling pin.

"Be my flour girl," he said. I sprinkled flour onto the dough every minute or so, pulling pans out of the oven and putting other ones inside in between.

John rested the rolled dough into three pie plates and put them aside.

He put a chicken in the oven, and we started peeling potatoes for shepherd's pie and mashed potatoes. Then he left while I was still peeling.

"Check this out," he said.

I turned to see him standing with three long ropes of dough on the rolling board.

"I thought we'd used up the dough," I said.

"Think again." He smiled, and started braiding up the dough so quickly it seemed like he was using a magic wand and telling the dough to braid itself.

I said, "John! You're a chef!"

"What have I been telling you?" he asked. "Okay, now we paint the top with egg whites and a shower of sesame seeds. . . ."

He put four loaves of braided bread into the oven. We dumped chicken and vegetables into the pie plates, pushing aside the lasagna to put in two shepherd's pies. Into another three pie plates (where did they come from?) he poured out something and threw in some broccoli.

"This is called quiche," he explained. "You'll like it when you're fourteen."

He poured something out of a blender into an old yogurt container. "This is pesto. Just thaw it out and throw it on spaghetti. I also made two kinds of tomato sauce, one with meat and one without. And they're both fabulous."

"When did you make that?" I asked.

"After you cut up the thirty tomatoes, silly. Remember?" Oh, that was right. He'd let me use the biggest, sharpest knife, something Joyce wouldn't have liked.

The bowls were all empty. So were the pots, with the exception of some soup cooking on the back burner.

The room was warm and it smelled wonderful. I looked around the counters and saw everything we'd made. Three quiches, two shepherd's pies, four loaves of bread, tomato sauce, pesto, meat loaf, a huge lasagna, mashed potatoes, and stuffing. And the soup.

It was midnight. It didn't feel so late, but here was the evidence of all our hard work!

"Thank you, John," I said, picking up a couple of pots to pack up for him.

"Thank me nothing. You're eleven years old, and you haven't asked about the most important part of dinner. We've got to make the dessert!" I looked over at the dozen eggs we still hadn't used. John started muttering to him-self and pacing around the room. "There are a lot of sad people around here. We need a lot of dessert. Get me the chocolate chips."

And we were at it again.

"Four cups of flour."

"Two tablespoons baking soda."

"Just pour the vanilla until I say when."

"All right, now separate these eggs, and when you're done, would you be an angel and pour me some wine?"

He had all the bowls going again. And the mixing bowl and a couple of saucepans simmering on the stove.

As I brought him his glass of wine, I saw it. It hadn't been my imagination.

John was doing the work of three chefs, whirling, toss-ing, stirring, and suddenly appearing with more food than we'd had to begin with. I was a little jumpy from the root beer, and I'd never been up this late in my life. The room was steaming from the heat of the oven and the simmering pots. In other words, we were a little deliri-ous, but something else was going on.

After the third batch of cookies and the second pie, I started to laugh to myself. John started laughing, too. I thought we'd used up all the eggs, and hadn't we been al-most out of flour?? Yes, we had!

"Look at these babies!" John cried, pulling five pans of cake out of the oven, two layers of chocolate, two layers of vanilla, and one "low-fat angel food cake, if anyone cares about their weight, but I don't think anyone does, especially right now."

We started frosting them, sometimes with John guiding my hand with the spatula.

"Thiiiis is how you do it," he said. "No use in your taking ten years to learn the right way, like I did."

"It didn't take you ten years," I said.

"Did too. I've always been a slow learner."

"Not true!" I said. "Dad said you were offered a scholarship to cooking school. But you turned it down."

"Well . . ."

"You went to regular college instead, and you made the food for everyone's parties and at all your friends' weddings."

"I'm a slow learner at business, then," he said, laughing.

"You should open a restaurant," I said.

"Of course, I'm going to. I've been telling you that for ages. I know I should. You think I should?"

"Yes," I said.

"You really think so? I mean, you're the best judge. I made all your baby food."

"Yes."

"Well, I'll be darned." He looked out the window over the sink. "That is a valuable compliment coming from you."

I looked out the window, too, and saw what was catching his eye. It was the sun.

Exhaustion set in as we loaded the dishwasher and scrubbed the counters.

"You think your dad's still asleep?" John asked, taking out a frying pan and scrambling the last six eggs.

"He might be," I answered. "The doctor said not to bother him if he is."

"Phooey. He's got to eat some breakfast if he's gonna get better. And we need a good breakfast, too," he added, dropping in some tomato and broccoli.

"John? Where did all this stuff come from?" I looked at the plates and pans that lined the kitchen, knowing there was even more food in the refrigerator and freezer.

"From the heart, Angel," he said. Then he saw what I saw. Breads, soups, pies, sauces, cookies, and cakes. "Honestly? I don't know. I've never done something like this before. I felt nervous about coming over here. Sickness scares me." He looked over to see if I could handle this. "But then I realized you all need my help, so I got it together and came over. And when I saw you two eating those peanut butter and jelly sandwiches on white bread, I don't know, something just snapped! I had some ideas of what to make, and then I had to make all of it! And here we are."

I was still wondering at John as he prepared a plate of eggs and added a small piece of coffee cake. "Breakfast dessert," he explained.

We walked down to my dad's closed door.

"Uh, Dad?" I whispered.

"Uppie uppie!" John cried. I jumped.

"I'm awake," came the voice from Dad's room.

"Oh, good, because we made you a little something." John swung the door open.

My dad looked so pale, I almost dropped his plate. John's hands fell and he looked at the floor.

"John made more food than we could eat in a year," I said quickly.

"Oh, good," said my dad. "I was worried about you!" I saw him brighten. "And I'd love a couple bites of those eggs."

John put on a good face. "No one takes just a couple bites of my eggs," he teased. "They only think they will. And then they ask for seconds!"

"That's always been the truth." Dad laughed, and he proceeded to eat a few bites, maybe four, and that was good enough.

"Now, if you'll excuse me," John said, as if we were at a little luncheon, "I've got things to do today. I've made some important plans."

I believed him.

CHAPTER SEVEN

Phyllis Talks and Talks and the Clock Goes Backward

"Merciful God!" as John would say. I made it through school on no sleep. John let me drink a glass of root beer at breakfast to give me "some pep." I slept a little in math without Mrs. Donaldson noticing and then napped in music class. Ms. Bernstein put her hand with its many jangling bracelets on my shoulder as I left the classroom.

She asked, "What did you see when you closed your eyes?" She thought I was concentrating on the Mozart CD she had played for us.

"Tall trees," I lied.

"Ahhh." She closed her own eyes. "I think Mr. Mozart would be very happy to hear that."

The next few days at school had a mix of bad and not-so-bad moments. For me, it was almost peaceful. Sure, Hally shook her head when I tracked mud into English class one morning, and Ms. Severance glared as I cleaned it up with a paper towel. She had been writing the word "ubiquitous" on the board, the word of the day. I'll never forget *that* word (it means seeming to be in many places at once).

But I'd also done well on the pulmonary system test. Since Dad and I weren't talking about anything serious these days, I at least liked to bring him good news, and this would make him happy.

There was also a new kid in school. I saw Ms. Severance through the window of the art classroom door, introducing the top of someone's head to Ms. Hutton, the art teacher. I could tell it was a girl, and that she had light brown hair, but I couldn't tell anything else. Was it better or worse to be entering school at the end of March? I didn't dare peek in to see, since Ms. Severance would definitely find something wrong with what I was doing. I winced a little as I heard Ms. Severance speaking so kindly to this new girl.

I was aware that time was moving along, whatever was happening. The world wasn't stopping for Dad's sickness. Even I was living day after day, though some days it seemed like school was a game I'd agreed to play while we waited for more news about Dad.

At home, I noticed there was something strange

about all that food John and I had made. It wouldn't disappear. I could eat a huge bowl of pasta and pesto, but the pesto container always seemed to remain full. I thought I couldn't eat enough cookies, but the jar was still so stuffed, I had to close it carefully.

Over the next week, during John's so-called shifts, he would make even more food — macaroni and cheese, tofu stir-fry, and chicken Parmesan. We never had any room to put the leftovers.

"Aren't you eating, Amalee?' he asked me one day.

"Yes!" I cried.

"Don't you make me worry about you, now," he drawled in his Southern accent.

I just shook my head.

Despite the fact that there was no shortage of food — particularly chocolate — all our spirits were starting to get low. There was no getting around it. Dad wasn't doing well. Dr. Nurstrom was learning how to break things to us more easily, but I don't think he was covering up the truth when he said that we should expect setbacks and that we shouldn't be discouraged.

Joyce was taking all the early morning shifts now, and she would nod her head and sometimes take notes as Dr. Nurstrom told her that my dad would be very tired, lose his appetite and sometimes fall asleep in the middle of a sentence. She said she enjoyed the nursing duties. She also enjoyed being around Dr. Nurstrom, and he seemed much happier these days, too.

In fact, after about two weeks, I wondered if Dr. Nurstrom was being irresponsible by letting Dad stay at home. Dr. Nurstrom obviously loved our house. Sometimes, he went jogging, and then he'd take a shower in our bathroom. At Joyce's urging, he'd started raiding the refrigerator every time he came over. I was relieved, of course. Somebody needed to eat all that food, and for a thin man, he sure could pack it away.

Dad started doing something that was so eerie, it felt unfair. It was one thing to keep us all in the dark about how he felt. It was another to start acting like we'd be better off without him.

"I'm so glad that John's made so much food," he said when I complained about the kitchen overspilling with cookies and lasagna. "It's great that everyone's taking care of you. They're doing a better job than I am!"

"Uh, wrong, Dad," I said, shuddering. He kept on saying stuff like that. The next day, he said, "Wow, my friends know all about you," and "Looks like you don't need me to make things run smoothly."

I was furious. If he thought he was going to die, he should talk to me about it. He shouldn't talk me *into* it, leaving me to hide my tears as I talked about math class, as if either of us really cared about multiplying fractions. I sobbed into my pillow every time I left his room.

But I couldn't bring up the subject. Dr. Nurstrom made it clear we shouldn't upset him. And besides, he was my father. It was his job to bring it up. Of course, I was also terrified.

I was a little surprised that Joyce didn't want to talk about it. I think she was afraid she'd cry too hard and manage to both upset and annoy me at the same time. I caught her looking at me a few times when I would say good-bye in the morning. She had put her hand on my shoulder once, out in the hall, and said, "How are we doing?"

Is it mean when you say something that you know will end a conversation, because you know it will leave the other person speechless? It probably is. I was definitely being squirrelly when I answered, "I'm okay. Everything's fine . . . right?"

Joyce did what I expected her to do. She took a little step back, took on the role of Dr. Nurstrom's unqualified nurse, and said, "Oh, yes. *Yes,* no surprises here, really. Uh, really."

"I wish Dad weren't in such a sad mood," I ventured. I did want to hear her opinion about this.

"Yeah," Joyce sympathized. "How does that make you feel?"

I didn't like that. I wanted information, not therapy! "He's probably just tired," I answered, not answering.

"He's very tired," she agreed. "He's healing."

She didn't say much after that, though I did catch her staring at me more.

At school, my secret became my shell. I hid inside it, looking out at the world. It was almost comforting. It was an excuse to be different and apart from everyone else.

A week or so after John had made all that food, I came home to Phyllis's car in the driveway. I was tired of this. But then I remembered that button Dr. Nurstrom mentioned, the one to summon me if my dad "couldn't breathe." Maybe it was okay that I was never alone with him. Also, I was learning that routines are the best way to keep living with all the questions no one could answer, so maybe all of these shifts and schedules were helping us.

Phyllis was actually looking relaxed as she sat on our living room floor, rifling through an old chest of stuff.

"How are you feeling these days?" she asked.

"I don't know, how are *you* feeling?" I asked, almost accusingly. She hadn't said anything about the latest downturn. Maybe Joyce had told her I hadn't wanted to talk about it. But what she said made me realize she wasn't exactly ready to deal with it herself.

"I am very hopeful," she said, "because Dr. Nurstrom told me this is about the worst stage of a sickness like this, and your dad is doing okay even without helping himself get better. But I was thinking, if we can convince him to get in more of a fighting spirit, I think it would be smoother sailing." I could tell she believed what she was saying.

"Your dad is depressed," she informed me. "And I have a plan." Ah, a plan. This was how Phyllis would respond to the latest crisis. She had surrounded herself with photo albums and yearbooks from her past with my dad.

"You want some lasagna? We've got tons of it," I told her, heading for the kitchen. I hadn't made a dent in it.

"Already had some," she called. "*And* some quiche, *and* some cake, *and* some root beer." She headed to Dad's room with her big pile of stuff. What was her plan, to bore him into a deep and restful sleep?

I stopped by his room on the way to mine.

"How are you, Dad?" I asked.

"Tired, as usual," he breathed.

"Okay, David. Sit up a little," Phyllis ordered. "We're going on a little trip."

"Where to?" he asked wearily.

"All over the place. First stop, the Adirondack Mountains."

Oh, wow. That was before I was born. Phyllis pulled out an album of pictures.

We all admired how awful everyone's hair looked. They were all about twenty-two. My dad's hair was severely winged back. John's hair was bushy and longer in the front than in the back.

"At least John *has* hair," Dad pointed out, laughing.

Carolyn, on the other hand, had almost no hair. She had a crew cut. Maybe she cut it herself!

"I'm lucky I was walking under the canoe for these pictures," said Phyllis. "I had the perm that made me look like a poodle."

"Oh, Phyllis, don't be hard on yourself," Dad said. "You looked like a springer spaniel." He chuckled.

Whatever Phyllis was doing was working. Dad shifted his pillows so he could sit up more.

I backed out of his room quietly, then worked on my math for a while.

There were swells of laughter and teasing coming from the other room.

I heard names and places here and there — the Catskill Mountains, high school boyfriends and girlfriends, and fifth-grade teachers.

Phyllis was always a big talker. Now she and my dad were going full tilt. A couple hours later, I went to the kitchen for some cake.

My dad's bedroom door was ajar. I walked past it, then I backed up, hearing how much their voices seemed to have changed.

They were looking at his pictures from summer camp. Dad was talking about how afraid he was every night, because the kid in the upper bunk told him he might get bitten by a rabid skunk. They talked about rabid animals, and how if one bit you, you'd have to get twenty-five shots in your stomach. My dad sounded like a kid who was still afraid of getting bitten, even though we'd been on lots of camping trips since then.

He said, "Do you like snakes?"

And she said, "Of course, I like snakes."

"Would you touch one?"

"I *have* touched one. At the zoo. With my dad. Would you touch a snake?"

"I don't know," said Dad, laughing like a boy. "I think I would at a zoo. But I wouldn't touch it in the real world, if you know what I mean. We had a snake in our basement one night, and nobody would touch it. It wasn't even poisonous!"

She said, "That's really scary! I mean, even if the

snake isn't poisonous, it could still bite you. It could crush you."

They both squealed.

The boy finished his story. "Anyway, my mom said my dad should deal with it, but he wouldn't, so she called the fire department." The girl laughed, and he went on. "She also called when there was a skunk, and she didn't wait for him to deal with it!"

They both continued to laugh. She imitated his mom. "Honey, really, DON'T deal with it!"

This was strange. I had heard this story before. But never like this.

I got closer to the door and heard the boy ask, "How did you get the name Phyllis?" I held my breath.

She said, "My grandmother. How did you get the name David?"

And he said, "My grandfather."

There was a pause, and then they talked about oceanography, and how they had always planned to make a ship out of unbreakable glass so they could always go below deck and see all the fish. Then Dad was giving Phyllis a lecture on what to do if she was attacked by a shark, as if we ever did anything besides swimming in lakes and creeks.

I was amazed at what Phyllis had done. She had led

him back so far into the past that he was opening up rooms full of childhood thoughts and memories he didn't even know he had!

He started yawning. "Hey, I'm really tired," he said, sounding surprised.

I saw him lean over and point to their high school yearbooks. "I really liked looking at those yearbooks," he muttered as he drifted off to sleep. "I remember when you got pretty. You went away for the summer before ninth grade, and you came back pretty."

Then my dad lay down and started to sleep, curling up and snuggling with his pillow as if it were a stuffed animal.

I backed away from the door so Phyllis wouldn't see me, but she flung the door open as she left his room. She was her full-grown self with her full-grown voice, wiping some tears away. "Amalee!" she gasped, as she closed the door. "Did you hear that?"

"I heard the whole thing," I whispered. "Why are you crying? You know you're pretty, Phyllis," I teased, but then I realized she *was* crying because of his confession that he thought she was pretty in high school.

"That's nice of you to say, Amalee. I just feel a little closer to fourteen than forty right now. And . . . and he never said I was pretty back then. He just stopped talking to me for a year. But that doesn't matter." She looked at the closed door. "Now I'm scared I've exhausted him."

"I'm sure he's fine," I assured her. For weeks he hadn't sounded as alive and excited as he had just now.

"I don't know what happened," she whispered back. "I just had a plan. I couldn't bear to see him so unhappy."

"I know. He's been acting like he's already a ghost," I said.

"Oh, no, don't say that, even if it's true," she muttered. I noticed her eyes welling up with tears again. "I know I talk a lot," she went on, smiling nervously. "And I know you think I talk a lot and that I'm sort of a busybody. Don't deny it. So I had this plan. . . . I thought I could talk him into remembering himself, remembering things that make him happy. I was so determined to make him happy again, I just kept talking and talking. And look what happened!"

"You made him happy," I said.

She clutched my arm. "Do you think I did?" Now tears were rolling down her cheeks. "Do you think I did something wrong? Did this happen because I talk too much? Sometimes I talk too much."

I knew how Phyllis felt. I remembered all those times Hally stared at me when I couldn't stop talking, because

I felt nervous. "No, Phyllis, you don't talk too much," I told her. "And you didn't talk too much."

Phyllis opened the door. There was Dad, half-smiling and fast asleep. We had no idea if he'd remember whatever had just happened.

Phyllis asked, "Amalee, did you see us, or did you see a *different* us?"

"Your voices were different."

"How different?

"If you don't know, I don't know."

Dad woke up about four hours later. Phyllis and I sat on his bed while he told us that he'd dreamed of fighting a snake and sailing in a glass boat surrounded by angelfish, barracudas, and sharks.

He seemed almost happy then. But in the days that followed, Dad looked terrible. He was sicker. Phyllis was panicked that she'd done something wrong, but I knew she hadn't. When Dad perked up at all, it was when I talked about jungles, oceans, forests, or even my social studies project on the first Thanksgiving. Phyllis had helped him clear a path to his childhood, and it made him happy whenever he went there. There was nothing wrong with that. Sometimes, I wished I could go there, too.

CHAPTER EIGHT

A Lot to Digest,
as Mr. Hankel Would Say

A few days later, Dr. Nurstrom showed up with what he called an intravenous bag, or IV bag, which meant he wanted to feed my dad with a tube. Joyce promised that she could check on Dad every four hours or so. She would be sleeping in the living room. Dr. Nurstrom was kind enough to tell me to look away while he put a needle in Dad's arm. That's how Dad would be "fed." I thought all eighty pounds of me were about to hit the ground in a faint. He put some tape over the needle, so I didn't have to see what was going on.

"Are you sure he shouldn't be in the hospital?" I prodded.

"Yes, but I need all of you to make sure the needle is in, not just Joyce. I'll be coming in twice a day, and you can use the beeper I gave your dad. It has my number, plus the number for Helen Forrest, a nurse who lives in New Paltz, and the one for Northern Dutchess Hospital." He stopped as if he'd remembered something. "Uh, tonight I can't come."

Joyce was standing next to him. "Why not, Robert?" I was surprised to hear her call him by his first name.

"Oh, it's just a little award ceremony."

"Are you getting an award?" Joyce asked, her eyes sparkling.

"Why, um, yes. It's an award ceremony for me."

"Well, well! This is an important night!" Joyce exclaimed.

"You could say that."

Dad suddenly spoke up, surprising us with the fact that he was awake.

"Could my friends go?" Dad asked Dr. Nurstrom. "They make a very good cheering section."

Dr. Nurstrom, or Robert, was trying not to look excited. "I'm sure they could come."

"Actually, the only person who can make it is Joyce," Dad realized.

"Well, in that case, I'll seat you at my table," Dr. Nurstrom said.

Was my dad creating an excuse for Joyce and Dr. Nurstrom to go on a date? Somehow this whole IV bag and needle thing didn't seem so scary if my dad was doing that! I was still scared, but I trusted Dr. Nurstrom more now, and I'd overheard him telling Joyce we just had to be patient for a while. I believed him. After all, he was an award-winning doctor.

At school, Ellen and Hally were unusually nice to me. Hally said she liked my sweater. I could have sworn she hadn't the last time I wore it. I think she said it was a peculiar shade of green that didn't quite go with my coloring. I would have stopped wearing it, but she had pointed out something wrong with all my clothes by now, so what choice did I have?

Ellen and I both went to our lockers before lunch. "Oh, no!" she moaned. "My lock is jammed again!"

"You can put your books in my locker," I offered.

"Thanks." Ellen rushed over. "Tell me your combination, so I can get my books later." I felt a little uneasy as I saw her write it on her hand.

She repeated, "Thank you *so* much!"

I'd seen the first robin redbreast of the spring on the way to school. I decided the new season was making everyone more friendly.

In science, something funny actually happened. It

was pretty awful, too, but I think Mr. Hankel should have expected what was about to happen.

He started the section on digestion. He pulled down a diagram.

We were fine for the mouth part. He talked about how digestion begins in the mouth, how saliva starts to break the food down. Then he ran his pointer down the esophagus, telling us about peristalsis, which is the rippling motion that pushes food down to the stomach. For the stomach, he even had a special effect. He pulled out a bone he said he'd soaked in vinegar to show the effect hydrochloric acid has in our stomachs. He bent the bone like it was made out of rubber. Interesting.

But things started to fall apart when he got to the large intestine. First it was giggling. We all knew where this was going. Then there were the obvious digestion noises every time Mr. Hankel turned his back. He started on the gallbladder, which wasn't even the bladder, but the laughing and the noises got louder. And then Mr. Hankel got so angry! I was a little surprised. How many years had he taught this? A million? He should have known.

He erased everything off the board and gave us a pop quiz on the parts of the ear. We were quieting down when we heard him mutter, "I don't know who got you all so riled up, but I'll get to *the bottom* of this."

Well, then even I had to laugh. The next five minutes were a chaos of sound effects, most of which required two hands, and then the bell rang.

It was not such a bad day.

CHAPTER NINE

A Very Crowded Breakfast

Dad had been on the IV for three days when I woke up to scratching and screeching noises down the hall. What would today bring? Dad's health, teachers, my so-called friends. Would things get better or worse?

I'd finally given up on talking to Dad about his real life or my real life. I was trying to live without anyone being able to answer any questions.

I thought maybe it was Phyllis making all the noise, so I got up. I actually liked our rides to school together, listening to her Broadway musicals. As it turned out, the noise was John. He was disappearing into my dad's room with a kitchen chair. Someone else came in the front door. It was Carolyn, with her short, freckly arms, sharp nose, and tight, thin mouth. I could see the small muscles in her arms as she carried in a painting easel.

"If I've parked out on the road, will I get a ticket?" she asked me. That was Carolyn, asking the person who couldn't drive. One thing I actually liked about her was that she didn't treat me like a kid. I think she forgot. I shook my head. No, no ticket.

"Do you have any coffee?" she asked, heading for the kitchen. "This is a little early for me." I nodded, then followed her into the kitchen to get some cereal.

"You want some?" she asked, pouring water for the coffee, and when she saw me with the cereal box, she said, "Good idea. Can you make me a bowl, too?" She pulled a couple of bananas out of her straw bag. "You can slice these on top."

I started talking with myself in my head. *Carolyn is bossy. That's okay. It's just what she's like. She brought bananas. That's a good thing. Say thank you.*

"Thank you," I said out loud, but I didn't like the way it sounded. It sounded aggravated.

John walked in. "Who wants eggs?" he asked. He saw me with two bowls of cereal. "Oh, well, *I* want eggs. And how about I make you a scrambled egg and tomato sandwich for school?"

I said, "Thanks, John. Sure."

"No problem. Hey, Carolyn, if you don't have enough coffee for me, your butt is seriously in the ringer."

"Oh, you want some?" Carolyn jumped up to make an extra cup.

"I help Carolyn lug her painting stuff into your dad's room, and she doesn't even remember to make me coffee," he groaned.

Carolyn didn't seem to hear him. "I'm going to paint a *trompe l'oeil* mural on your dad's wall," she said.

"What's that?" I asked.

"It's French for 'fool of the eye.' You paint something so realistic the eye thinks it's real. I could paint the lawn and the sky outside his window, and you would think that I'd just knocked down the wall."

"You're that good?" I asked.

John turned and gave me a look. I looked at my cereal.

"Oh, yes," Carolyn said, matter-of-factly. "But I'm not painting the lawn. I'm painting an enchanted garden." She strode out, with John about to follow. He had two plates of eggs.

"Who's the second plate for?" I asked.

"For your dad, silly! Could you bring us some juice? I'll come back for the coffee."

"Haven't you heard?" I asked. "He hasn't eaten in three days."

"No!" John looked unsteady. "Oh, Lord, I saw the IV bag, but I thought it was, you know, vitamins or something. I don't know anything about this. I've hated all this medical stuff since my mom died in a hospital." He stood and considered the eggs. "I'm just going to wave this under his nose. And then I'll eat it myself."

I got ready for school and visited Carolyn, John, and my dad as I was leaving.

"How are you, Dad?" I asked.

"Just tired, sweetheart," he answered with a half smile. "John's got me propped up, so I'm going to watch Carolyn paint. Then I'll sleep, I'll watch, and I'll sleep again."

"I'm taking care of your father today," Carolyn pronounced. This worried me. She had offered me a cup of coffee. What would she do to my dad? I saw the real possibility that she could knock him out with paint fumes and so I cracked the window open with a thin book that Carolyn had brought.

"Hey, I was going to read that to him!" she said. "It's about the effects of acid rain on the indigenous cultures of northern Quebec. Stunningly written. Real cultural resonance and sensitivity."

"That sounds very uplifting, Carolyn," said John. "But I agree that the window should be open, and besides," he said, winking at me, "I know the way you work. Once you start, you're unstoppable. Your talent has a mind of its own."

"That's true," Carolyn agreed thoughtfully.

I kissed my dad and winced when he said, "Be good." It was only last year, when I was in the fifth grade, that he would say, "Be good," kissing me on the top of the head. I would say, "And what is good, according to philosophy?" Philosophy is the study of everything good and bad, right and wrong. He would say something like, "Well, this philosopher says don't drop your history report in the snow on the way to school, and we can call that good. Wait! That's me telling the day to be good for *you!*" I would laugh, and so would he. Things had really changed.

I walked out of Dad's room with John, who started laughing as soon as we were in the hall. "Oh, man, acid rain? What was Carolyn thinking? How about some good bedside reading?" He went on, "And it's a good thing your dad has that IV bag. Carolyn can't make toast. But she *is* good at lettering."

He nodded at my lunch bag. She had written my name on it in a beautiful medieval-looking script.

"Have a good day," said John. "Don't let the mean kids get you down."

How could I even begin to tell him that *I* was one of "the mean kids"?

CHAPTER TEN

Carolyn's Masterpiece

School was a blur of misunderstandings from start to finish, like getting in trouble when my pen ran dry and I couldn't find another one.

First I was stared at for rustling in my book bag, and then I was "separated" when I asked Ellen if she had another pen. She just gave me a blank look. So much for being on her good side. Luckily there was a pen on my new desk, the only good thing that happened in school today.

Lenore pestered me about whether I wanted to sleep over. "My mom says you have to tell me yes or no. What are you doing next Friday night?" I'd already told her I couldn't come this week.

"My aunt is coming," I told her.

"What about Saturday?"

"She's coming for the whole weekend."

"I could come over."

"She's taking me fishing," I said.

"In March?" she asked.

"Uh . . . she's from Canada." What a pile of lies. I had no aunt, let alone one from Canada.

"Oh, okay then," she said. "Sunday?"

"No," I said, and walked away, out of lies.

I ate lunch alone backstage. I looked at my lunch bag, with Carolyn's beautiful writing of my unusual name. Inside was the egg sandwich, and I could tell it was made with care. Carefully cut in triangles on lightly toasted bread, with just the right amount of salt and pepper. Even the tomatoes weren't soggy. John also put in an apple and a big piece of cake. Maybe he knew how much I hated school, or maybe that's what he always did for people.

We studied the arrival of the French in North America in social studies, and that was cool. They came through Canada, trapping beavers and otters as they paddled on the St. Lawrence River. They weren't like the settlers who came with a religious mission. They just wanted to hunt and fish and make a lot of money. They lived rough. I thought of my made-up aunt from Canada who was going to take me fishing in March. I thought about her all the way home.

*　*　*

The first thing I saw when I got inside was Carolyn standing outside my father's room. "I don't know what came over me," she said, almost shaking. "I thought this would take a few days, but it's — it's done! And it's quite extraordinary!"

She didn't seem as sharp as she usually was. In fact, if there was one word to describe how she was acting, it was shy — shy about whatever it was she'd done.

She looked me in the eye. "Amalee, I'm very good, but this is different." How could I tell her that something very different was going on for all of us? She hadn't seen John working in our kitchen, where sometimes it looked like he had more than two arms. She hadn't watched Phyllis zooming herself and Dad back to childhood to help him forget his sadness.

"Do you want to see?" Carolyn asked.

We went into the room. I didn't know what to say. I expected a wave of paint fumes to hit me as we walked in, but instead I could almost smell what I can only describe as the color green. I smelled moss and leaves and long grass because they were right there in front of me. Plants whose stems were as thick as celery, with huge shiny leaves and large drooping flowers, plush green grass leading into a hedge, and slightly off to the side, a giant gnarled tree with silvery branches spreading out in a spiral over carpets of tiny white flowers and violets. Under its branches was an archway.

I looked over at Dad, who was sleeping, no surprise, and turned back to Carolyn's incredible creation. As I walked closer to the painting, I saw the garden continuing farther in. On the other side of the archway were ancient-looking fruit trees, with all their peaches, apples, plums, and apricots catching the soft, golden sunlight. The trees grew in fields of tall grass and wildflowers, and when I stepped forward, I could make out the beds of small white flowers in the distance beyond. That's when I walked into the wall.

"That's a wall," Carolyn said, in explanation.

"Thank you," I replied sarcastically.

She wasn't making fun of me, of course. That was the great thing about Carolyn's seriousness. She would never make you feel stupid for believing something that wasn't real. She might have walked into the wall herself and realized, as I did, that the wall was less like a wall and more like a blanket of warm summer air, and that it smelled like grass.

I stepped back and clapped my hand to my mouth.

"I know," Carolyn spoke in a whisper. "This isn't my work. It's better than me."

We both looked at the garden again. I saw more things. In the wildflower field, there were flowers that looked almost like fireworks, and others that looked like big floppy bells.

Carolyn stepped forward and stood with me, close to the painting. "I think I see what happened," she said under her breath. "You see, I kept on painting and painting, but the flowers seemed too small. There they are, over there." She pointed to tiny distant flowers. "And then I thought, *No, fields full of wildflowers. That's what I'll do.* And I thought, *No it's still not enough!* And I painted a hedge over the whole thing, with an entrance you could see through. But the hedge was too heavy and too boring, so I painted flowers in front of it, but it still wasn't enough! This is your father we're talking about! This wasn't good enough for him! And I thought, maybe a big, ancient Japanese maple, and then maybe rubber plants and rain forest plants, big Amazonian plants, maybe that would be dramatic and beautiful. Beautiful enough."

"And look at it," said my dad. "The enchanted garden."

We both swung around and saw him, wide awake.

Carolyn still looked like she couldn't believe it. "I guess so," she whispered.

Then she bent over and took something out of her straw bag.

"David," she said, anxiously, "I got you something." She straightened up, brushing something off. "Would you like an apricot?"

In her hand was a small apricot, glowing deep yellow, almost orange, rosy along the side. It looked warm from the sun.

I felt myself almost wanting to yell at her. Hadn't she listened to anyone? He couldn't eat! That was the problem! I also shot a glance over to the painting, where the apricots on the trees looked exactly like the one she was holding out. They were so similar, I almost wondered if this was enchanted fruit, if Carolyn had wandered into the garden just long enough to pluck one ripe apricot from the tree.

"C'mon," she said, extending the fruit to him.

My dad took it. He closed his eyes and smelled it, and then he took a bite. I held my breath. He took another bite. He almost finished the apricot.

"I thought you'd like it," she said quietly.

He tried clenching and unclenching his fingers. Carolyn put a bunch of sprigs in his hand. "Chew on these. This is milk thistle. It's for your liver. And this is the root of a purple coneflower, echinacea."

Echinacea? That sounded like a monster from a Greek myth, one with six heads.

"It's for your immune system," Carolyn explained. "And Saint-John's-wort. For depression."

My dad chewed a little on each, then said weakly, "Nice of you, Carolyn, sleep . . ." and he fell asleep. I wasn't sure if that meant it was time to remove the IV bag.

He looked okay. I could even see a little color in his skin, as if he had a little of the sunlight on the apricot inside him.

Carolyn and I walked out as his eyes started to close.

"I'm discovering something," said Carolyn. "I think I — like making people happy. I mean, everybody likes to make people happy, but it never seemed to work with me. I don't know why."

Poor Carolyn, with her mysterious paintings. She'd been speaking in code for as long as I'd known her. I always thought that Carolyn, from the planet of Carolyn, with the secret language of Carolyn, was saying, "Look at me!"

Well, sure she was. But today I saw that she'd been saying something else the whole time. She'd been saying, "Can't anybody see that I care?"

Carolyn was mostly quiet as she ate two helpings of pasta with pesto and some vegetarian meat loaf. She didn't believe in the phrase "uncomfortable silence." I'm sure silence was very comfortable to Carolyn. She liked a lot of time to think.

When she left, I peeked in on Dad, then skidded over on my socks to the phone. I hadn't wanted to hurt Carolyn's feelings when she was at our house. But what had she just done?

Joyce answered the phone on the first ring. "Are you all right?" she squeaked out, knowing it was me.

"I think so. It's just that . . . Carolyn got Dad to eat."

"Did she? Wow."

"Is it really 'wow,' Joyce? I mean should I take out the IV-needle thing?" I tried to sound calm.

"I'll call Dr. Nurstrom and get back to you right away, Amalee," she answered, and I'm not sure if she sounded grateful for the trust I placed in her, or for the opportunity to call Dr. Nurstrom.

The nurse, Ms. Forrest, came by in about an hour and spent some time in Dad's room. "He's really weak," she pointed out. "I think we should keep him on the IV for the weekend. Did he ask to eat?"

"Uh, no," I answered honestly. "His friend really wanted him to eat something, so he did."

"And he didn't throw it up?" she asked gravely, as if I wouldn't tell her if my dad had thrown up! I shook my head.

"I took care of him," said Ms. Forrest, adding that I should just let him sleep tonight, and that she was always on call.

Still, I lay awake waiting for his little beeper to go off, letting me know that there was an emergency. Or, at least, I thought I was awake. I found myself walking down the hall, into Dad's room, and up to the painting, which was still full of sunlight, even though it was close to midnight. I saw the leaves of the rubber plant move a little. I saw wind blowing through the wild grass, bending the fragile stems of the violets, then, finally, blowing the red leaves of the tree upward to reveal their white undersides. As I smelled the violets and felt the wind in my hair, I heard laughter behind me.

"You're just a kid!" my father said, laughing, as he moved beside me.

"It's true," Carolyn said, standing next to him. "You're a kid. That's a fact."

I realized I hadn't felt like a kid for a while. Dad nudged me forward. "Don't you want to go in?" he asked. I held out an arm and walked straight, right into the garden. Dad and Carolyn were following behind.

"Can you climb up there?" he asked me, pointing to the Japanese maple.

I looked at Carolyn. Could I? Did she paint a strong tree?

"The Japanese maple is a very dense hardwood," she said. "The branches are like iron."

I started climbing up the tree. It felt like a staircase that you climb with your arms as well as your legs.

When I was about ten feet up, I looked down at my dad. He was laughing. I went up another few feet and out along a big branch. There was Carolyn's world, Carolyn's gift to my dad, fields of wildflowers, fancy flower beds in S shapes, circles around ponds, orchards and hills of soft grass blowing to the south.

"Hey there!" Dad called. "We've got to get going! The sun's going down!"

I joined them at the bottom, and giddy from our time in the garden, we turned to leave. Carolyn leaned over and whispered, "Relax, Amalee. Some things are a mystery. Isn't that wonderful?"

Then we stepped out of the garden and into the room. And then I woke up.

CHAPTER ELEVEN

The Good, the Bad,
and the Much Worse

I was relieved it was the weekend. The week in school had its moments, but I liked the peace of having a full weekend to do my homework. Dad's friends were more . . . predictable than anyone at school.

Phyllis stayed for the whole weekend, checking in on Dad, who did not eat again, but who clearly felt better. John dropped by on the way to the bank on Saturday morning, very excited about something, but when I asked him what was so exciting, he just said, "Life. Life itself, my little daffodil."

Monday morning arrived. It was April Fool's Day, but in the morning, there was no joke, just a good feeling in the air. Dr. Nurstrom came very early and took out the IV.

"I don't understand it," he said. "But it happens often

enough. You don't need this anymore. I just can't believe you are so ahead of schedule. You're accepting the drugs better. It looks like your liver is functioning at a much higher level than it was last week, and overall, your immune system seems to be working more smoothly."

He shook his head. I thought of the roots and twigs Carolyn had given my dad for his immune system, his liver, and depression. Did he seem less depressed to the doctor?

As if he were reading my mind, Dr. Nurstrom said, "You're in better spirits, too, and you have better color." He reviewed his charts. "I haven't changed anything. The only explanation for this progress is my undeniable charm."

Dr. Nurstrom cracked a joke? He must have, because my dad smiled. Dad turned to me and said, "Amalee, could you make me an egg?"

"It's remarkable that you want to eat," the doctor said.

"I know," Dad told him. "I wish I could have eaten John's eggs the other day. He put the plate under my nose, and I wanted to eat them — as much as I wanted to throw up!"

Oh, gross! I started out of the room. "Do you want two eggs, Dad?" I asked.

"No, just one."

Everything was turning out better than expected this morning, and all I could do was shake my head and laugh.

I brought my dad the egg, made myself a scrambled egg sandwich, took an apple and a big piece of cake, and headed off for school.

I got to my locker and panicked. I had no pens or pencils, and my English and social studies notebooks weren't there.

"Idiot!" I said out loud. Everything crashed down. I was so angry at myself. Ms. Severance would hate me. I was so busy playing in enchanted gardens and thinking about my dad's doctor that I left my notebooks at home! I could have sworn I hadn't even brought them home, just the books and assignments, but I must have.

I went to English class. Ms. Severance looked at me with a cold eye. I was a minute late. "As I said, please take out the test I handed back on Friday. Let's go over it."

I had nothing. I opened my science notebook to take notes. Then I saw an anatomy test in the folder. I unfolded it and pretended it was the English test, my stomach looping into bigger and bigger knots as Ms. Severance strolled toward my desk. I was able to hide the test the first time around. I pretended to be checking some other notes in my notebook.

I did this again the second time she came to me. As she circled my desk, I looked straight down at my notes, and then I heard, "That isn't my handwriting."

The bottom of the anatomy test was sticking out.

"Amalee, what test are you looking at?"

"Science," I said. A few kids laughed.

"That isn't funny," said Ms. Severance.

"No," I said. "I left my English notebook at home."

"So you didn't come to me at the beginning of class — oh, that's right, you were late."

I wanted to scream out, *"Please! You're the only teacher I like. Why do you hate me?"*

I couldn't say anything. I looked over at Ellen and Hally. They were laughing behind their hands.

I was in shock all through math class. Whatever good happened in school, there was always the bad lurking around the corner. School was just a house of needles, always about to collapse. Every day, I felt a little pinprick underfoot, a reminder that it was all about to fall apart.

That day at lunch, I looked down at my bag. I'd lettered it myself, trying to make it look like Carolyn's handwriting. It looked sloppy, silly. Then I heard a rustling sound. In the darkness, I saw a figure. It was another girl. I watched her stand in front of the ropes that drew the curtains.

She tucked her long hair behind her ears nervously, and then she ran her hands down the ropes, nudged her foot against the sandbags, looked up at the lighting beams, and finally looked over at me.

"Oh, God!" she whispered, surprised to see me.

"I won't get you in trouble," I said.

"Oh!" She clutched her heart. "I did theater in my old school. My mom says all theaters smell the same, so I should come smell the new stage."

"Does it smell the same?" I asked. I watched her relax a little.

"Yeah, it does, actually," she said, laughing a little. "I guess it smells like old costumes and dusty curtains." She banged on one of them. We both coughed.

She stood for a second. She had light brown hair. It was the new girl. For one moment, we were perfect strangers, perfectly nice and perfectly well-meaning. I already liked her. I liked the way she looked at things and the way she beat the curtain. I liked the way she liked things that didn't have to do with people.

"I'm Sarah," she said. "Sarah Smythe."

"I'm Amalee," I said. "Amalee Everly. As you can see, I really like the cafeteria."

I held up my lunch.

"I understand," she said. "I think all cafeterias smell the same, too."

"Here, you have to try this." I reached into my bag for John's cake. I couldn't believe what I felt at the bottom. There were two pieces. Even though I had packed the lunch myself, I could hear John laughing in my head, saying, "Honey, I just know when you're gonna need a little extra!"

So we sat there and ate our boulders of cake, and then we disappeared.

I forgot about Sarah during science class, realizing I had social studies next, again with Ms. Severance. And no notebook for that class, either. Science was a long walk from social studies. I always had to run just to make it on time. And today, of course, there was a teacher behind me. "No running!" she said. "And I'm going to walk behind you to make sure you walk." I walked quickly for a while, and when she went into her classroom, I started to sprint. And that's when I tripped.

Everybody thinks boys are mean, but it's girls. Their laughter echoes more in the hallway. Nobody helped me up, nobody helped me with my books. Nobody asked if I was okay. My knee hurt. I was late for social studies. This time it was a surprise quiz, but we were allowed to use our notes, if we had our notebooks, of course.

I wrote an answer for every question, even if it was just a guess. I looked up and saw Ms. Severance frowning at me. She didn't wish me well, no matter how hard I was trying.

After class, I heard a voice behind me.

"Amalee, wait up!" It was Lenore. "Can you stay at my house this Friday?"

"I already said I couldn't."

"Well, that's just the thing. My mother says you're lying."

"I'm what?" I didn't stop walking.

"She said she doesn't believe you have an aunt from Canada. She says you shouldn't lie to people." Lenore was panting as she tried to catch up with me. If I could just get to the stairs, go down the stairs, through the door, into the woods — "She said you should be grateful when someone offers to help you." We were close to the top of the stairs. "And she says," Lenore sounded very smug and victorious, getting right up behind me, "that your dad is dying."

She knew.

And it was as bad as I'd thought. My shell of secrets was broken, and the mean words and anger were all swooping in, like birds who like to punch their beaks into eggs so they can suck everything out.

She stood about an inch from my ear, breathing. I swung around and pushed her away from me. And then she was nowhere. Behind me was open space. I had pushed her down the stairs.

She yelled as she went down, hitting her head once and crumpling at the bottom.

Other kids came to the top of the stairs. I started running down.

"You pushed her down the stairs!" someone yelled.

"You killed her."

Hally and Ellen joined the crowd.

"What have you done?" Ellen cried out like a bad actress in a worse film.

She looked like she was going to faint.

Hally pulled something out of her bag, looking disgusted. "Here!" she yelled, throwing two notebooks down the stairs. English, social studies.

Lenore sat up and batted paper away from her. "Lie down," I said.

The nurse was already there. "She's right, lie down," she said. "Is this the only place you hit your head?"

"Yes," said Lenore. "She pushed me."

"It was an accident," I said.

Lenore looked me straight in the eye and said, "I'm going to sue you for all you're worth!"

"Okay, okay," the nurse interrupted, "we're calling an ambulance, and if you promise to lie very still, maybe I'll call your lawyer." She shook her head and shined a flashlight in Lenore's eyes. "Take the other staircase!" she yelled up to all the kids. "Everything's fine. We had an accident. The buses are waiting. I mean it!"

The crowd scattered.

"You go, too," she told me. "She'll be fine."

I didn't think I should go. "Go!" the nurse ordered.

I snuck out the side door, hid behind the school, then cut home through the woods, watching the ambulance lights bounce off the trees. The loud voices on the walkie-talkies followed me all the way home.

I walked through the front door and immediately heard my dad's voice. "Hey there!" he tried to call out.

I rushed to his room, so he wouldn't hurt his throat. He was sitting up with a small bowl in his hand. "Who made this soup?" he asked.

"John did."

"That's not what he told me," Dad proclaimed, smiling proudly. "He just left. He said you made all this stuff with him. It's excellent, Honey. John certainly has more bounce in his step these days. Have you noticed? I told you he wasn't angry at you."

It was no good. Sure, I helped John with the soup. Sure, he wasn't angry at me. But soon we'd get a call from a lawyer, saying we'd have to sell the house. For all I knew, Lenore was dead, and my father was next. This would kill him.

My father saw that I was unhappy.

"Hey, guess what? I feel better! I really do!" I thought about Lenore's mom. How did she find out about Dad? She worked at the bank. I could just imagine Joyce and John talking about it within earshot of Mrs. Nielson. And now, if one person in school knew, everyone knew.

"That's great that you're feeling better, Dad," I said. "I'm just thinking about all the things I have to do."

"Oh, of course. Well, could you get me that book over there before you go? Phyllis brought it for me. It's about the Congo. You know what's amazing?"

"No, what?"

"Gorillas. I can't get enough of them!"

I knew why Phyllis had gotten him that book. She was helping him on one of his paths to recovery. He was seven years old again when he looked at these books. Dad's friends had done amazing things, and I was about to undo everything.

I hid in my room and couldn't do any homework. Later that night I brought more food to my dad. "Hey, Amalee, do you want to eat together?" he asked. It would be the first time since he got sick. I turned away as I started to cry. I wanted to give him, and me, the gift of one whole, almost normal dinner together.

But I couldn't eat. I said I'd already had dinner, and he looked disappointed.

I lay in bed that night, thinking of all the things I should have done.

Why couldn't I just say, "Lenore, you're right. I lied. I just didn't want to stay at your house"? Why did I push her? I knew better. Why didn't I talk to her?

I woke up around three in the morning. Had somebody tied me down? My arms were stuck to my sides, and my stomach was so clenched up it hurt. I could barely breathe, let alone move. I wasn't a good kid who had done a terrible thing. I was terribleness itself, trapped and frozen in this thing that I couldn't take back.

Everything I loved was about to disappear, and it was my fault.

I didn't go to school the next day. I kept on freezing up again in the morning. I still couldn't eat. I told my dad I'd come down with something.

"Well, I'm a little sleepy," said Dad, "so you can borrow the gorilla book if you want."

That was a generous act for a seven-year-old.

I skimmed through the big pictures and wished I were a gorilla. I felt every minute of the school day. It was slower than school.

At around two-thirty, Phyllis came over. She had two big books for my dad, one about Madagascar and one about iguanas. "Stay here, Amalee. I'll be right back." She brought the books in to my father who thanked her enthusiastically.

Then Phyllis came out and sat down at the kitchen table. "Sit down," she said. "You're in trouble, Amalee."

I sat and looked out the window. Now I'd lost Phyllis. She had heard the news. She didn't like me anymore. None of my dad's friends would after this. Even Dr. Nurstrom would be angry. "I'm sorry, Phyllis," I started.

"You're not in trouble with me," she said, surprising me. "You're in enough trouble at school. I want you to tell me why you did what you did, but no matter what, I want to help. I don't want your father to find out. Have you told him yet?"

"Of course not," I whispered.

She pulled some papers out of an envelope. "Rumor

has it that the school wants to suspend you for a week and give you detentions until the end of the year. Lenore came to school in a neck brace today, and I've heard she wants to sue you, or your dad, of course." She stared at me. "There's got to be another side of this story, Amalee. You have to tell me what happened."

"I deserve it," I said. There was silence, broken only by my dad turning an oversize page in his room.

"Amalee, you could have killed her!" Phyllis exclaimed. "Please tell me it was an accident."

"It was," was all I could say.

John liked to say, "Merciful God," but right now, I was grateful to Merciful Phyllis. She relaxed a little, as if I'd given her enough information, when I knew she wanted more of an explanation.

"How can I keep this from Dad?" I asked.

Phyllis shuffled the papers back into the envelope. "Here it is. I came up with a plan. I called him from the office today. He's going to sign a form saying that I can give you permission to do things. Dr. Nurstrom will sign it, too. Your dad thinks this is about permission slips to go to the city with your class and stuff like that. You can stay with Carolyn while you're being suspended. She's at home applying for jobs next week."

"What jobs?" I asked.

"Haven't you heard? Carolyn wants to work at a gardening store. I don't know what happened here last Friday, but she got very excited about planting things and landscaping and medicinal herbs. She keeps on saying she knows this will make people happy."

I couldn't help smiling a little.

"I can drive you home after detention most days of the week," Phyllis continued. "Usually, I stay late at school anyway."

"That's really nice of you, Phyllis."

"I'm more worried about this legal thing," she said. My stomach sank. "But you know what? Here's the good news, kiddo. I met with the nurse today, and she gave me some information. She said she overheard you saying it was an accident, and she confirmed that Lenore didn't even have a concussion. Things could be worse. Also, I met Lenore's mom once. She brought in a late permission slip. She was perfectly nice."

After what she'd said about my dad? Yeah, right. I wished I could ask Phyllis about how Mrs. Nielson found out, but then I'd have to tell her everything.

"You really have to tell me what happened," Phyllis repeated.

What was there to tell? I pushed, and she fell.

❧ CHAPTER TWELVE ❧

Standing in the Bad Guy's Shoes

I had to finish the week at school. I would fail if I missed two whole weeks.

If it got really bad, I'd hide backstage and listen to the gym classes killing each other at dodgeball.

I almost left after English. Lenore's neck brace was attaching her head to her body, or at least that's how it looked. When she first saw me, she seemed frightened, pointing at me with a trembling finger.

"I'm really sorry, Lenore," I said.

"My lawyer said you'd say that," she pouted.

"I brought you some cake and lemonade, with a straw." I put them on her desk. "Do you need anything? Pen or pencil?"

This is what I knew: *Don't make a bad situation*

worse. I'd prepared myself in the morning, bringing extra things for Lenore.

"It'll be hard to eat cake," said Lenore, obviously wanting some. "Where do you eat your lunch, anyway?"

I hated to lie again, but there was no way she could find out my hiding place, especially now that the secret was out about my dad. "We don't eat at the same time, remember? A few of the A-team kids eat with the C kids because we're all in the same music class."

Lenore watched as if all the words were buzzing out of my mouth. She was clearly confused. "That's right," she murmured.

I looked around and saw Ellen and Hally staring at me with disgust. "Don't talk to me, okay?" said Ellen.

I looked away. Their April Fool's Day joke was so cruel. But they hadn't pushed anyone down the stairs.

I just told myself to keep surviving.

I was prepared for the kids, but not for Ms. Severance. She wouldn't look at me, even when she handed out some photocopies.

I said, "Thank you," but she said nothing.

I had an unusual thought then. It was a thought that was sticking up for me.

If Ms. Severance read about me in a book, she would

have sympathy for me. We'd already read about a person who shot his best friend, and about an evil king, and a woman who locked her child in a closet. After the class was through saying that each of them should die a terrible death, she'd always smile, hold up a finger, and say, "Now, put yourself in this person's shoes."

I had used her words with people inside and outside of books. Ellen had dyslexia. She was always embarrassed when the tutor took her out of class. I knew that was part of the reason she'd stolen my books. She liked to watch other people squirm the way she did. When I put myself in her shoes, I wasn't as angry at her. I felt sorrier for her.

Lenore had started wearing a bra in the fourth grade. I knew she felt like a freak. Her mother always made her wear thin white blouses, too, so everyone could see her bras. Everyone could snap her bra strap and run away. She wasn't the only one this happened to, but she didn't seem to notice this. She thought she had to force people to be friends with her. She never let people choose to be her friend, because she was sure they wouldn't.

Was I worse than everyone else? Was I so atrocious that even Ms. Severance refused to walk in my shoes?

I lifted up my chin and looked at Ms. Severance. She caught my eye, and I didn't look away. She lost her place in a sentence. *Good,* I thought, *if you have a place in your heart for killers and haters, I have to believe you have a place for someone as awful as me.*

People yelled things at me in the hall, but no one spoke to me all day, except Mrs. Donaldson, who said, "Amalee, I have a note here that says you should go to the principal at lunchtime." The whole class turned and looked at me.

Someone said, "Good." I felt all the hatred in the room focused on me.

Mrs. Donaldson looked like she couldn't care less about the note. She was a gorilla who had lived in the jungle for a long, long time. I stared straight ahead as she started multiplying fractions on the board.

The principal, Mr. Shapiro, told me what Phyllis had already said.

Suspension, detention. He didn't look up. Unlike Phyllis, he didn't want to hear my side of the story, even if I'd had one. He just shook his head and said, "What are things coming to, little girls beating up little girls?" I guess he understood it when little boys fought. Weren't they supposed to punch each other in the jaws and break each other's arms? Actually, I didn't know any boys who had. I was more violent than a boy! Now, who was the freak of nature?

I left Mr. Shapiro, an old, white-haired man, bent over his notes like Father Time recording the long sad history of little girls turning bad.

I didn't see Sarah. Did she go backstage during lunch again? Did she think I didn't want to see her? Maybe she didn't care.

In science, somebody left a note on my desk that said, "You are a mennis to sosiety." Despite the really bad spelling, I cried a little, but I straightened up before anyone noticed.

Finally, there was social studies. I got there in time. Ms. Severance handed back my test. Something stood out. With a red felt-tip pen she'd written the score, 88. But then in red ballpoint pen, she'd written, "This is very good work, especially without your notes." I knew it. I could just tell.

She'd gone back this morning and written something nice on my test. She'd put herself in my shoes.

CHAPTER THIRTEEN

Dad's Friends Want to Save the Day . . . for Me This Time

The next day, I wondered if things would start getting better. I saw Hally in the morning.

I said, "Hi,"

She said, "Hi," and rushed away.

I stood near Ellen at the lockers. All she said was, "I can't believe what you did," and shook her head, as if she had been my friend once, but not now that I'd betrayed her.

"I'm sorry about it," I said. "I really am."

She shook her head again. "I just hope the judge believes you." She sighed before walking away.

Lenore came in before class. I'd brought her more cake, but she said, "My lawyer says I can't talk to you."

Ms. Severance said she'd had a migraine headache

last night, and she was still feeling "woozy." So the day was not off to a good start.

Lenore walked down the hall with Hally and Ellen, which almost made me laugh. Ellen was so desperate to make me feel bad that she was being nice to the girl who annoyed her the most. Then I thought of Lenore telling them about my dad, and I felt clenched up again.

Some boys were behind me. Otherwise, the hall was empty. The girls had gone downstairs. Was it my imagination, or were the boys talking about me?

"Amalee can't go to jail, but her dad can."

"What about her mom?"

"Her mom ran away. They can't find her."

I didn't want their sympathy, but I turned and said, "My mother passed away."

"What, did you push her down the stairs?" asked Jimmy Whitman. The other guys looked a little surprised.

"No," I said, so shocked that I couldn't think of anything else to say. We were getting close to the stairway.

"Maybe I'll push you down the stairs, just so you know what it feels like." Jimmy kept on going. The three boys were close behind me.

Tommy Fallon said, "C'mon, Jimmy. . . ."

"C'mon what?" Jimmy turned on Tommy. Then, as I

got to the top of the stairs, he nudged my shoulder. I almost lost my footing.

"You're a psycho!" Jimmy shouted, racing ahead of me down the stairs with the other boys. "Loser!"

I just froze. I didn't care if I made it to math. I wasn't sure I could ever leave this spot.

I heard a voice behind me. "Are you okay?" It was Sarah Smythe.

"Yeah," I said.

"He's awful," she said. "He's in my art class. I saw the whole thing."

When I was silent, she said, "I'm sorry. I'm sorry I didn't tell him to stop."

I felt the beginning of tears. Was she afraid of me? Could I ask if she wanted to eat lunch backstage again?

"That's okay," I said. "He's scary. Scary for both of us."

"Yeah." She looked uncomfortable, and then she said, "We'd better go to class."

I felt like I had a remote control in my hand, and I was trying to find the button that would make my legs walk. I started down the stairs, slowly. "Yeah, let's go." I agreed, trying to sound casual.

"Guess what? I'm going to be in a play," she said. "I got in."

"Bye Bye Birdie?"

"Yeah, I'm Kim," she told me. "It's the lead."

"Wow! That's great. Congratulations."

"I thought of you when I was auditioning on the stage. I hope it means you can still eat back there. You know, in the backstage."

She talked about *me* eating backstage, not *us*. So I guessed that was her answer.

"Oh, don't worry about me!" I assured her.

Every time I sat down and stood up, I had to remember how to make my legs work, how to keep moving through this day. I tried not to think about my dad or kids talking to me about him.

In social studies, I hoped Ms. Severance would smile at me, but she didn't.

And with that, I decided the day had been a complete failure.

I was surprised when I got home. Carolyn, Joyce, Phyllis, and John were all sitting at the kitchen table.

"What the hell is going on?" Carolyn wanted to know.

If it were just Carolyn, I might have told her. She was always ready for anything.

"Carolyn!" John moaned. "She's just a kid! Don't ask questions like that! Here, Honey, I made you some orrecchiette with pesto, and I heated up some eggplant Parmesan." I guess John forgot I was a kid, considering his menu choice, but then he pushed a plate toward me. "Or do you want to skip right to the cookies?"

"*I'll* skip to the cookies," Phyllis said.

I couldn't eat. "You're not eating," Joyce observed. "Amalee, when you can't eat, it usually means that you're ashamed of something, like you feel you don't deserve to eat."

John said, "Joyce, if you start crying, I might start, too."

"I can't help it," she sobbed, wiping her eyes on her sleeve. "This poor kid. What terrible thing could she have done that she doesn't think she deserves to eat? I'm sorry." She got up. "I've got to get back to the office anyway. You hang in there, Amalee." She rushed out to her car.

John got me some pasta, and he, Phyllis, and Carolyn all started picking at it with forks.

After a few minutes of silence, John said, "Well, Ama, far be it for me to pry something out of you. I'm sure whatever you did is not as bad as you think it is." He got up to go to work and added, "You know, Phyllis and your dad had the same principal as you when they were in middle school. She says your principal is an idiot."

"John!" Phyllis cried.

"But she can't tell you that, because now she works in his office!"

He laughed and skipped out the door.

"I don't think anyone's an idiot. That's an unkind word," Phyllis told me and Carolyn.

"But do you like him?" Carolyn asked, not realizing, as I did, that Phyllis was trying to be a role model.

Phyllis looked at me, and then at Carolyn.

"The principal is very good at . . ." she started. "I mean, his intentions are . . ."

Wow. She couldn't even think of something nice to say about his intentions.

"He believes that obedience and order are very important." She shot me a look, "And they *are,* of course. It's just that sometimes things are out of order and I believe — this is just me — that it's valuable to ask *why* they're out of order, rather than just forcing everything back *into* order." She looked miserable.

Carolyn asked, "What do you mean?"

"Well, here's an example," Phyllis pressed on. "We've had budget cuts, which means when the middle school got more students, we had to hold some classes in those drafty outside rooms we rented." I could see Phyllis starting to get upset as she explained. "Suddenly, I noticed a lot more students going to the principal because they were always late or caught running more than once. Some of them even had skinned knees!"

Hey! Phyllis knew what I thought only the kids knew, that our school was too big for us to get anywhere on time.

She continued, "Clearly these kids were late because they didn't have time to get to class! That made me upset. You'd think Al Shapiro would poke his nose out of his office, or maybe just care enough to ask students why they were always late, but you know what his explanation was? He just thought the kids were getting lazy. I mean, it didn't even occur to him to get more information!"

Carolyn snorted. "Is he one of those guys who says that American kids are slower and fatter than they used to be?"

Phyllis groaned. "Basically, yes. He's believed that ever since I was in school, and he's only gotten worse." Then she widened her eyes. "Oh, Amalee. He's a good man, don't get me wrong."

"I won't tell on you," I promised her.

"Oh, no, it's not that," Phyllis protested. "Well, maybe it is."

"I won't say a word," I repeated. "But I agree with you."

Carolyn looked at me. "So your principal doesn't understand kids, and you've got some whiner going around pretending she's going to sue you. John's right. Phyllis said all this to us, even if she won't admit it to you. That's what Phyllis said."

"Oh, Carolyn, honestly . . ." Phyllis said. "Look, let's give Lenore a break. She's just a kid."

"So is Amalee!" Carolyn shot back. "The nurse said this kid was fine, so what is this lawsuit thing about? She's threatening Amalee! Whose side are we on, anyway?"

"Maybe she feels threatened by Amalee," Phyllis suggested quietly.

"Oh, c'mon, Phyllis, we know this was an accident," Carolyn answered.

"Well then *she* should tell us," Phyllis said, looking at me.

"It doesn't matter if it's an accident. She is going to sue me," I said.

They both stopped and looked at me.

"Tell us what happened," Carolyn pressed.

"No."

"Tell us," she said.

"No."

"It can't be that bad."

"No!"

She took a breath. "When I was ten, I left my little sister in the car. My mother told me to stay with her, but I wanted a chocolate bar, so I went into the grocery store where my mother was shopping, and I bought one. It was the summer. I left the windows rolled up almost all the way, and my sister really, truly almost died. Okay? Now tell us what happened."

Well, that was awful. Should I tell them?

Suddenly, Phyllis jumped in. "Amalee, I kicked your dad in the shins when I was twelve, because I had a crush on him and he was being mean. He had to go to the hospital. I guess I kicked him harder than I thought. I was nervous," she added, still defending herself.

"Pretty mean," said Carolyn.

"You almost killed your sister! For chocolate!" Phyllis protested.

"I pushed Lenore down the stairs!" I shouted, interrupting them. "She hit her head! I heard it. It was awful."

"Aha, okay, was it on purpose?" Carolyn asked immediately.

"Of course not. I pushed her, but I didn't even do that on purpose."

"Why did you push her?" Phyllis asked.

"Because she wanted me to sleep over at her house."

"And?" Carolyn wanted more.

"And I'd already said I couldn't, and she wouldn't stop asking."

"So you were annoyed, and that's why you pushed her?" Phyllis asked.

"Well, I was already upset, because Ellen and Hally had stolen my notebooks as an April Fool's joke."

"Not funny," Carolyn observed. "Go on."

"And I was really upset about it, and then Lenore wouldn't leave me alone, and then she said this thing."

I paused for a moment. I didn't want to repeat Lenore's words.

"What thing?" Phyllis asked suspiciously. "What thing did she say, Amalee?"

"This thing where she said her mom said . . . that I should be grateful to go over to their house since Dad is . . . is . . . dying."

There. I told them. I started crying.

"Did she just say what I think she said?" Carolyn asked Phyllis. "It sounds like Mrs. Nielson said that David was dying, and Lenore said it to Amalee. I guess Mrs. Nielson found out somehow. I know John was at the bank last week. He might have told her," Phyllis said, sighing.

"So, John gave her the news, but then she told her

daughter? No way!" Carolyn exclaimed. She and Phyllis were both so upset, they didn't even get up to put their arms around me, which was fine. If they hugged me, I'd have to pretend that I didn't feel so alone.

"I don't know about Mrs. Nielson, but that Lenore is a mean child!" Carolyn stormed, on the verge of tears — something I'd never seen. "Are you sure you didn't push her on purpose? I would have!"

"Look, it wasn't okay what she said," I explained, trying to stop crying. "But I've been avoiding her all year. I've been walking around letting everyone think I don't like them and not saying anything when people are mean to people I like. I've been awful."

"Wait a minute, Amalee," Phyllis said, stopping me. "Are you saying you deserve what she said, because you think you're a bad kid?"

"Um, yeah. That's why I didn't want anyone to know about Dad. I knew they'd get back at me for . . ."

"For what?" Phyllis asked impatiently.

"For changing. I used to be nicer."

Phyllis tried to disagree. "People won't punish you for that. Sweetheart, I don't know why Lenore would say something so mean —"

"Because she's the devil," suggested Carolyn.

"Stop it, Carolyn! Amalee, you shouldn't expect people to be so cruel."

"But they have been. It's true," I explained. It was the simple truth.

"This is so upsetting," Carolyn said. "First of all, your dad's not going to die, but we've been on pins and needles about him. I can't believe someone would make you *more* worried." She pounded the table in exasperation. "We've been tiptoeing around, saying, 'What about Amalee? Should we talk to Amalee? Is David going to talk to Amalee?' And this kid just waltzes in and says, 'Do what I want you to do or I'll tease you about your sick dad.' We should have pulled you out of school. I would have given you painting lessons."

"We've been a little worried about you," Phyllis confessed.

I started crying again. They had been worried about me? They knew I was having a hard time, and I didn't even have to tell them. They'd been watching out for me.

For once, Carolyn talked to me as if I were more her daughter than a friend. "We're sorry, Amalee," she said. "We're sorry that we haven't insisted on talking to you about your dad. The thing is, we don't know what to say, and we told Joyce not to get too . . . you know, like a therapist. But, well, I feel like a jerk. We should have insisted that you tell us how you were feeling! We should have taken care of you better."

"You think you haven't taken care of me?" I asked. "Of course you have. And it's not like I've made it easy for you."

Carolyn nodded her head and smiled, grateful that I'd let her off the hook.

Suddenly, Phyllis stood up. "Okay, it's official. I've got to do something."

CHAPTER FOURTEEN

Phyllis Talks Again,
and the Clocks Go Forward

Phyllis grabbed her coat. "I've made a decision," she said. I almost thought she was angry at me, she was so decisive. "You're getting in my car, and we're going."

Where?

"C'mon," she insisted, getting her keys and her purse. "We've got to go before I lose my nerve."

"Where are we going?" I called out as we ran to her car.

"I am not going to let you be bullied. You made a mistake." She started the car. "I'm forty-two years old, and I'll act like a parent if I want to." She *sounded* like a twelve-year-old. "Let's face it —" she couldn't stop talking now — "your dad isn't dying, but we all had a good scare. And we didn't know what to do. And we didn't know how to talk to you about it, because, well, you're eleven, even if you act older, and we didn't want to upset you. . . ."

"You did the best you could. . . ."

"True enough, but in the end, we were very confused. We just felt helpless." She took a deep breath. *"Helpless."*

That was a huge word for her. Phyllis had never been helpless. She could be very unhappy, but she always, always had a plan. A plan to get her car out of the muddy ditch last spring, a plan to teach me multiplication (she wrote an equation in removable marker on every bathroom tile), and a plan to make the vegetable garden grow (it still didn't).

"But you aren't helpless with Dad!" I exclaimed. "You've helped him so much!"

Phyllis was silent for a full minute.

"You know, we have. Maybe that's why I have the courage to do this now. I'm not like Carolyn. I don't dislike Lenore, but we've got to set the record straight. You've gone through your father's sickness with almost no help from us. You're not going to do *this* alone."

We pulled up to Lenore's house, where Phyllis had dropped me off a few times. Strangely enough, I almost felt better about seeing her house now than I had when we'd called ourselves friends. I'd always hated going to her house. At least now, it was out in the open that Lenore didn't like me. Not that I wanted to go in the house at this moment, which was Phyllis's plan.

"Let's go," she said, heading for the front door.

My first reaction was to push down in the seat, like a dog that won't go to the vet. But she walked with so much confidence, I only felt a small wave of dread as I jumped out and followed.

Phyllis gave the knocker two loud raps, then stood with her arms folded.

"Your father is going to be fine," she repeated. We heard footsteps approaching. "But Lenore didn't know that. I don't want to be unkind about her, but I am really angry about this. Man, am I angry."

Then the door opened, and I watched Phyllis's straight back sag a little, as if she suddenly wasn't so fired up. Uh-oh.

"Hi, Mrs. Nielson," she said to the woman with peering eyes and short brown hair.

"Yes?"

"I'm Phyllis Francisco. I work at the middle school. We've met."

"Oh. Is this . . . school-related?" Mrs. Nielson asked. "Would you like to come in?"

"We'd love to," Phyllis replied. Mrs. Nielson jumped a little when she saw me.

"Amalee! Is this about . . ."

"Lenore and Amalee, yes," Phyllis answered. "Can we sit down for a few minutes?"

"That's not a good idea —"

Phyllis interrupted, "I only went to one year of law school, but I know you can't hurt your lawsuit if you don't say anything. And also, we want to help."

We sat down at the dining room table. Phyllis had gone to *half* a year of law school.

"And one more thing," she added. "We want Lenore to be here, too."

I slid down in my seat. Lenore appeared from behind a door that I could have sworn was to a closet.

"Hi, Lenore," said Phyllis. "Thank you for sitting down with us."

Lenore looked at her mother, and her mother looked at me as if we'd never met.

Phyllis continued, "Amalee doesn't think this matters, but" — she paused — "I think it's important for us to know that she was having a hard day. This happened at the end of the day, right, Amalee?"

I nodded. What was Phyllis doing?

"So at the end of the bad day, you, Lenore, invited

Amalee to sleep over at your house, and for some reason, which we can only guess at, she ended up pushing you. I know you can't speak, but I imagine that felt unfair, scary, all those things."

Mrs. Nielson spoke up. "It was. She went to the emergency room. It was expensive, and our insurance won't cover all the things we need."

"Well, Amalee should definitely pay for the rest. You don't need a lawsuit for that," Phyllis said. "I just wanted you to know that this was an accident."

"She pushed me!" cried Lenore.

"She did, but she was trying to push you away from her, not down the stairs. And she didn't even mean to push you. It's just that when you thought she was lying, well, you know, that's hard, especially since she *was* lying. She doesn't want to sleep at anyone's house right now, and she doesn't want to invite anyone over, mainly because her dad is sick."

I expected Lenore to look over and call me a tattletale, but she was looking at the ground.

"And so here she was thinking she was protecting your feelings, and I think" — Phyllis looked at the ceiling as if she were consulting God, and then she plunged in — "I think when she heard that you thought she was lying, and even that she should be grateful for an invitation, because some people think her father is dying . . ." She was looking at Mrs. Nielson now.

"Oh, Lenore!" Mrs. Nielson stood up. Mrs. Nielson was the one who had told her daughter my dad was dying. Now she knew her daughter had passed along her prediction. Lenore looked surprised and embarrassed. Actually, so did Mrs. Nielson.

"I think Amalee was just trying to get home, and she didn't know what to do," Phyllis went on. "I think Amalee didn't mean to push you, Lenore."

"Of course not!" Mrs. Nielson said.

Phyllis went on. "You and Lenore must be very concerned about Lenore's injury, and I am concerned, too. And I know Amalee is very sorry."

"I am," I said.

"Never mind that," Mrs. Nielson muttered. "It's not the point, obviously." She stood.

Phyllis and I got up and headed for the door.

"David Everly is expecting to pay any bills you have," Phyllis said.

"Tell David to concentrate on getting better. And how is David . . . ?" Mrs. Nielson started.

"He's doing much better, thank God. That's the good news. He's doing better every day. I would not say that he's . . . in trouble anymore."

"I'm so glad to hear that," Mrs. Nielson said, and I knew she meant it. "And I believe it. I'm sure the last thing anyone needs is loose gossip about his health."

"Well, you know, we try to take everything in stride," said Phyllis.

I could tell Mrs. Nielson was trying to apologize to Phyllis. "We weren't going to actually sue anybody. We were just talking to a lawyer. I wasn't trying to make any trouble."

"Of course not. I can certainly understand your concerns about money. It's a crime what those insurance policies *don't* cover, don't you think?" Phyllis was being chatty, trying to change the subject. She must have known that things weren't as bad as Lenore was saying at school.

Now Mrs. Nielson turned to Lenore, who was trying to slink out of the room.

"Don't move," she told her daughter. Then she bit her lip and turned to me. "Amalee, how are you doing these days?"

"I'm fine," I said. "And I am so sorry. I should have known better. I'm sorry, Lenore." It felt good just to say it.

"No, Amalee, we're sorry. We're very, very sorry."

CHAPTER FIFTEEN

Ms. Severance Teaches
Her Most Important Lesson

And so it was Friday, my last day of school before a week of suspension.

I walked into English class early. Only a few kids were there. Ms. Severance was leaning up against the desk, her back turned. She was talking with Phyllis.

Phyllis stopped talking when she saw me.

Ms. Severance swung around and said, "Hi."

"Amalee, come outside for a second," said Phyllis. She took me around the corner. "I don't want Lenore to see us talking. She must be so embarrassed."

"Embarrassed?" I said.

"Trust me," she said, "you're not being suspended, you're not getting detention, and I can't imagine anyone's going to sue you. Mrs. Nielson called the office this morning."

"Wow," I said.

"I agree! Listen, I've got to go, but . . ." Phyllis shuffled her papers around. "I, um, I've never been a mother before. I don't know if I had any right to do what I did yesterday. It's just, well, everybody gets to tell their side of the story. I believe that, and I just wanted to be efficient. I wanted to find the most direct way for you to tell your story. That's all I was thinking. Are you angry at me?"

I was stunned. "Why would I be angry at you?"

"Because I sort of ratted on you last night, you know, by repeating what Lenore had said to you about your dad."

"I know why you did that, Phyllis," I told her.

"You do?" she asked.

"Yeah, you wanted to clear the air."

"Exactly!" she said.

"And it looks like it worked."

"Whew, yes, I was relieved," she said. "It looks like Mrs. Nielson is nervous about the hospital bills, and they thought they'd need a lawyer to get the money from us."

"How much will I owe them?" I asked.

"Nothing, I think. Mrs. Nielson is raising three kids alone. She doesn't have time to read all her insurance information or call the insurance company four times a day. I'll do that for her. I think she's covered, though."

"I could give them money. I could earn it for them," I protested.

"It would probably be about five hundred dollars," Phyllis warned me.

I sucked in my stomach. "That's a lot of lawns to mow," I said, "but I could do it."

"Sit tight for now. If she's still got that neck brace today, we'll know that she has some real neck problems, and we should offer to help," Phyllis agreed. "But if she doesn't have a neck brace, we'll assume that she's okay, and you won't have to mow lawns for eight hours a day. Fair enough?"

I nodded and asked, "Phyllis, you know what I liked the best? I mean, do you want to know how I really feel?"

"How's that?" she asked.

"I feel forgiving."

"That's nice," Phyllis said, surprised.

"I forgive myself, I think. I forgive Lenore, her mom, Mr. Shapiro."

"And me?" Phyllis asked.

"You didn't do anything wrong."

"You don't know what I did this morning," she muttered. Then she confessed, "I told Ms. Severance about your dad. I told her everything. I broke my promise."

"Why did you do that?" I gasped.

"Because she's a new teacher, and I like her, and I thought she could help you if I told her some of the things new teachers don't always know."

"She doesn't like me," I protested. "She thinks I'm a bad student."

"She likes you, Amalee. She likes you a lot."

I felt like I'd just eaten one of the apricots from Carolyn's enchanted garden.

"I like *her* a lot," I whispered.

"Well, if you can trust that I broke my promise for the right reasons — and, by the way, I felt like I could because John had already spilled the beans, obviously — if you can forgive me, I think you're also going to be asked to forgive someone else."

"Who's that?" I wondered.

"Ms. Severance."

Ms. Severance?

I walked back into class and sat down. I couldn't even look at Ms. Severance. Then Lenore walked in. The neck brace was gone. She looked much smaller. She didn't look at me or Ms. Severance. She didn't look at anyone.

The bell rang, and Ms. Severance was silent. We waited for her to speak.

When she finally did, it had nothing to do with the

word of the day or grammar. She said, "When I came here, a year ago, I thought this job would be fun, because I think learning is fun. When you know more things, you understand more things, and you can do new things. In that way, learning gives you power."

Her voice was quiet and steady, as it always was, but she seemed a little nervous.

"But when I started teaching," she continued, "I don't know how it all happened, how things changed. I had a few kids in my class who were bullies. They made fun of me and the other kids. I was truly surprised. All I wanted was to help them learn all this great stuff, and they wanted to fool around and make fun of people.

"So I went and spoke to an expert here at school, and he said I had failed my students. He said it was my failure, because I hadn't given my students enough order. He said my class was in chaos. He said I shouldn't have expected to have fun. I shouldn't have thought we could laugh and enjoy learning together. He said I had to be strict, and that the biggest gift I could give my students was order, structure, and seriousness, because then nobody could misbehave, and I could get my job done."

This sounded familiar. I put two and two together. She was talking about Mr. Shapiro, the principal. I bet that Phyllis had been in here this morning telling her she didn't have to listen to him! I realized he had said all these things to Ms. Severance and made her feel unsure of herself. Poor Ms. Severance, trying her hardest to be orderly and serious, when she really wanted to be nice. Phyllis must have gone ahead and told Ms. Severance what all the students knew, that Mr. Shapiro was a loon.

"I think the expert was wrong," she was now saying. "And I think I even hurt some students in the process, because the other piece of bad advice he gave me was this: If you have one or two very able students, students who have a strength in English and social studies, you should be the strictest with them. If they think they're smart, they will get conceited. They must believe they haven't tried hard enough yet."

Her eyes only flickered in my direction, but I caught the pain in them.

Somehow this was the Ms. Severance I had been wanting to see all year, the one who went with the beautiful mossy green sweater and the sparkly earrings.

Now things made sense — her cold looks that went with my good grades, the fact that she never smiled when I answered a question correctly.

"The truth is, you are a fabulous group of students, and you've learned more than I ever thought you could in one year, and I think you deserve to know that. So, congratulations! Now, on to the word of the day."

Everyone looked happy, even Lenore.

I was afraid of getting too excited as I left Ms. Severance's class that day, but I dared to think that now I could be happy about waking up and coming to school. I could show up for Ms. Severance. I could let her know how much I loved the books we read, the words she taught us, and even her North American history assignments.

And now that the Lenore nightmare looked like it was coming to an end, what about the rest of the picture? Did I have any friends? Did Sarah still like me? It's easier to forgive than to ask for forgiveness. But she never seemed to be mad at me. No, I didn't have to ask her to forgive me for what happened with Lenore. I just had to talk with her.

I saw a girl named Marin walking down the hall. She was friends with Sarah. Here was an opportunity. I would talk to her. If I wanted friends, I'd have to find a way to be a friend.

"Marin," I almost whispered as she passed.

"Did you say my name?" She stopped and looked at me.

"I — I saw the stained-glass project your team did in

art class," I stammered. "We're doing them next week, and Ms. Hutton showed us the one you did as an example."

"The ones our class did, you mean?" she asked, one eyebrow raised.

"No, the one you did by yourself. She showed us all the details on it and said it was one of the best ones she'd ever seen. Did she tell you that?"

"No," Marin said shyly.

"Well, it was really good," I said, starting to walk away. Clearly what I had said made Marin uncomfortable.

"Wait!" she called, then caught up with me. "I'm friends with Sarah Smythe. We're in *Bye Bye Birdie* together. She told me about what happened, and she said — Lenore Nielson told her why you pushed her."

"She did?"

"Lenore knew it was because she said your dad was really sick." Marin looked away and murmured, "I felt bad for you. So did Sarah. We thought we might have done the same thing."

"You put yourself in my shoes," I said. "That's what Ms. Severance always says."

"Yeah."

"I don't usually push people," I added.

"I didn't think you did! How is your dad feeling?" she asked.

"Much better," I said. "Thank you for asking."

We headed off for our classes. I didn't even care if I was late.

CHAPTER SIXTEEN

Joyce Takes Us on an Unexpected Journey

My books were lighter as I walked home from school, and the sun was shining through the trees in the woods, like an enchanted forest to go with Carolyn's enchanted garden.

I was excited to see my dad. Maybe I'll tell him the whole story. Okay, maybe I'd tell him *most* of it. And, I thought, I would talk to him about his being sick. He had avoided the whole conversation with me, but I would bring it up with him. I would ask him everything about it.

He was sitting in the living room reading the paper. I sat next to him on the couch.

"Hey, there," he said, smiling. "Did you have a good day at school."

"I had a great day," I answered. "How are *you*?"

"I'm fine," he said. Silence.

"Well, that's new," I encouraged him. "After the couple of months we've had."

"Hey," he said, "Phyllis says she's gotten you up to speed on the government. Did you know we've got a big election coming up this year?"

I couldn't speak. It hadn't been my imagination. He refused to talk to me about his sickness.

"Do you really want to change the subject?" I asked.

"I was just asking if you knew about the election in November. It's earlier than that, actually. The primary in September should be pretty big, too. Do you know what happens in a primary?"

"Yes. People from the same party run against each other and the winner runs against the other party in November." I spoke as flatly as I could, just to show him that two could play at this game. No feelings.

Then I got up and said, almost threateningly, "I have to make a phone call." Dad just nodded his head and went back to his paper.

I called Joyce and left a message.

She called back before dinner. I pretended she was someone from school, just to experiment with this idea that to be a friend I had to act like a friend. I told her I felt frustrated. I told her I needed her advice. I knew now that I was determined to do things differently. I told Joyce about Phyllis and Ms. Severance and how I felt about it. She'd already heard about Lenore from Phyllis. Then I swallowed and told her about Dad, and how he still wouldn't talk about anything but the September primary.

"So you'd like me to help?" Joyce asked.

Did I?

"Yes, I'd like some help with this," I said.

"I'm proud of you, Amalee. I've been hoping you'd ask."

"Why are you proud of me?"

"Because you're like your dad sometimes. You don't like to talk about your problems, and you don't like to ask for help."

"Isn't that just what human beings do?" I asked, a little afraid. I didn't know other people had noticed this about me.

"Why, yes!" Joyce said. "But you know what I mean about your dad. He's not exactly John. Or me." She laughed.

I got off the phone when Dad walked in the room.

"So who's running in the September primary?" I asked as seriously as I could, heading toward the kitchen to get us some vegetarian meat loaf for dinner. We could talk about politics over dinner. I would be happy to be eating with Dad in the kitchen, and I'd let Joyce take care of the rest for now.

*　*　*

School was starting to feel much better. After lying low like a river rock for the last two months, I didn't feel the need to hide or to be so hard. I sensed that there was another river, next to the river of unkindness. It was the river of kindness, of course! It didn't make the loud rushing noise of mean words and accusations, but was, instead, often quiet, and maybe harder to find.

Hally had a hole in the armpit of her sweater, and I didn't point it out like I knew she would have. Who cared about a little hole? Not we who swim in the river of kindness!

I could survive the kids who were hard to deal with now that I trusted that there were kids who were trying to be nice.

Lenore tried to talk to me about our next social studies project. She started to explain that she'd picked the most difficult subject, but too much had happened between us. She couldn't boast the way she used to. She knew that she shouldn't have been mean about my dad. She knew I felt like a monster for pushing her the way I did. Competing over history projects was nothing compared to our own history.

I overheard Ellen telling her latest victim that George Washington became president in 1789, not 1776. I watched Bob, a pretty serious kid, nodding his head respectfully, ready to accept her suggestion that he was a little stupider than everyone else because he didn't know it took over ten years for the United States to end the revolution and elect a president.

When Ellen walked away, I said to Bob, "I didn't know that about George Washington. I thought he was elected on July fourth, 1776, when they all signed the Declaration of Independence!"

"So did I," he confided.

"I guess we're not very smart," I said sarcastically.

"Oh, yeah, me and the smartest girl in the class," he joked. Is that how the other kids saw me?

Ms. Severance was almost dancing as she wrote the words of the day on the blackboard. She asked for a sentence with all three words.

Bob raised his hand. I felt like I'd given him a little lift.

"Excellent!" Ms. Severance cried. He had used the words "opaque," "transparent," and even "translucent" correctly.

Bob looked up and then down at his notebook. He didn't know where to look. This was very new for him.

Ms. Severance had clearly gone and talked with some other teachers, because in music class, Ms. Bernstein put the words "Lachrymose: tending to cry easily or to make people cry" on the board.

"Here's a vocabulary word that you'll probably never use!" Ms. Bernstein announced cheerfully. "It comes from the Latin word *Lacrima* 'tears.' I wanted to play you one of the most beautiful pieces of music I've ever heard. It's called the 'Lacrymosa,' from Mozart's *Requiem*, which means *'music for the dead.'*" We all shuffled around a little when we heard this. "By the way, Mozart was writing 'Lacrymosa' when he knew he himself was dying," she added, "so it is truly a lachrymose piece of music. Feel free to let a few *lacrimae* go."

Did she choose this because of me and my dad? She slipped a CD into the player.

This was different from the symphony she'd played a few weeks before. The violins played slowly, as if a very sad parade were passing by. I felt the tears starting to well up. I thought about a man who knows he's going to die and who thinks about the way things come to an end. Is that how Dad had felt? Yes, lachrymose, indeed.

That day, after school, I saw Joyce's car in the driveway. I wondered if something had happened. I plopped down my books and got a few cookies from the kitchen. Then I made my way to Dad's room, only to see him sitting up, his back perfectly straight against the pillows on his bed.

"Oh, hi," whispered Joyce, sitting next to him.

Joyce looked a little nervous.

"Hi, Amalee," she said, moving over so I could sit between her and Dad on his bed. "Your dad has just agreed to let me try an exercise with him, something I read in an excellent book. It would really help me if I could practice it on him. I told him it's just a little something to stretch his brain."

"I said I would be happy to be a guinea pig," Dad said innocently. Somehow I suspected that this wasn't just an innocent exercise. Joyce was up to something!

Joyce looked down at me and smiled as if I'd just read her mind. Then she cleared her throat and said, "Close your eyes, then." Dad and I both closed our eyes, even though this — whatever it turned out to be — was for him. Joyce continued. "Think about something that is filled with water. Think about that lovely red vase next to your bed, David, the one that Carolyn has filled with flowers. Think about the bright red vase and how it contains water so perfectly. Think about the vase without the flowers. It's just a vase with clear water inside."

Every sentence ran as smoothly as water into the next sentence. It was beautiful. I never knew Joyce could sound so calm and soothing. The next things she said were just as watery and floaty, but they came out as very separate things to ponder.

"Now think about all the things that a person can cry about. In fact, think about all the things you yourself might cry about, things that are gone that you cannot change, or, on the other hand, things that are very, very beautiful. And now, think of a moment in the last couple months, say, when you may have felt like crying, but you thought that if you did, you might never stop."

Joyce took an extra pause here, and found another way to say the same thing. "Somehow, you thought if you started to cry, you would think of everything in the world that makes you cry." She paused again. I was trying to think of what my dad might be thinking. "Now," she said, "imagine a big rubber stopper, like the stopper in a bathtub, and imagine pulling and pulling on the ring handle. You finally pull it up, and suddenly a fountain of tears comes welling up from a deep hole in the ground. What container would hold all those tears?"

After a minute or so, Joyce asked, "David? Do you see a container?"

"I'm in a boat," he answered. "I'm in a boat on the water." I'd always heard that some people were easier to hypnotize than others, and judging from the sound of his voice, I guess Dad was one of them! He sounded so different, it was strange, even though it was a relief not to hear the forced cheerfulness I thought I'd been hearing for the last few weeks. This was working! This was actual hypnotism! Was Joyce allowed to do this?

"I'm in a red boat on the water. It's a rowboat. And it's raining. It's very cold, and it's raining!" Dad's voice was rising.

I felt something very strange then. It was a cold gust of wind at my neck, even though the window was closed, and I thought I could smell the rain — almost feel it. I saw a flash of red somewhere out in front of me.

Suddenly I saw myself on a beach surrounded by the plants that Carolyn had drawn, as if I'd gone back into the dream I'd had about being in her garden.

But I was in a part of the garden I'd never seen before. I was on a beach, and rain was drumming on the big green leaves of the rubber trees behind me.

In front of me was the water. I could smell the salt in the air. It was the ocean. An ocean of tears! And Dad was alone in an old red rowboat with chipping paint. He wasn't that far away. I waded out and then swam to the boat. The water was warm, but the rain was freezing and falling in angry little daggers. Somehow, without Dad seeing me, I slipped into his boat.

He spoke again. "I'm shivering, and — and — this is terrible!"

He was shivering. I could see him. But he still couldn't see me.

Joyce spoke so gently, it seemed normal that she wasn't actually in the boat with us. She was simply a presence. She asked, "Are you afraid? Think a little deeper, David, what does this rain remind you of?"

Dad was almost yelling, because the rain and the waves were getting louder. I started shivering, too.

"I feel exposed!" he cried. He was trying to answer the question, which made me feel proud of him, to my surprise. He was talking about how he felt. "I — I am cold and alone, and no one can help me. What's going to happen to Amalee in this cold, driving rain if I can't even help myself?" My breath caught on the sound of my name.

Joyce didn't rush to make him feel better. Instead, she went a little farther into what he was saying. "So you feel like if you don't get better, you'll run out of money, you'll lose your house, and your daughter won't have anywhere to go?"

"Yes — that is *exactly* what will happen," Dad said loudly. I wanted to touch his hand and say I could take care of myself, but I knew this was not the time. I kept my arms wrapped around my chest in the freezing rain, watching the cold water drip from his hair onto his neck.

"David, you're forgetting something," Joyce almost cooed.

"What?" he yelled.

"You're forgetting something very important."

"My bank savings?" he asked.

"No, David. Well, yes, you have some money squirreled away and, sure, that could help. But, David, . . . think about what else you have. Think about . . . your friends."

"They'll get sick of helping me! I can't put this on their shoulders!" he insisted.

"David," Joyce said firmly, as if she wanted to raise her voice. "You have listened to John talking about his big plans until three in the morning almost every week-end since college. That's twenty years. You have bought an endless number of Carolyn's paintings, even when she did that horrible series about her knees. You listened to her describe every one of them, too. You helped Phyllis get a job after her divorce." He did? "And me. Well, I don't want to go into what you've put up with. But you know."

"It didn't feel like I was helping you. You're my friends."

"Well, how do you think *we* feel?" Joyce asked, trying

to keep the soothing tones in her otherwise exasperated voice.

The wind gradually died down in the silence that followed. The rain became a cool, April mist, and then it stopped completely.

"Has the rain stopped?" Joyce asked.

"Actually it has," Dad said in a humble voice. Clearly, Joyce had stood up to the voice of his fear, which we all knew was no small feat.

"All right, then. If we're on an entire ocean, there are bound to be other things that come up. David, do you see anything?" I caught myself looking around at the calm ocean. I couldn't see the shore, which was a little frightening. Joyce was right. This boat wasn't coming in to shore yet.

Dad wasn't ready to come home.

"LOOK!" Dad cried. I jerked my head.

"What is it?" Joyce asked.

It was rising just above the surface, whatever it was, and coming at us faster than we could outrun it. I thought I might throw up, I was so scared. Dad's expression didn't make me feel any safer. He looked terrified.

"It could be a shark!" he cried.

"A shark," Joyce repeated firmly, but calmly. Obviously she couldn't see it.

It was coming so fast the boat was starting to rock.

"Yes! A shark, which is dangerous, and cruel, and doesn't care about me, and — and —" Dad was looking hard at the smooth, black shape that we could now see under the water as well as above the surface. He was trying to describe his fear so that Joyce could tell him how to make it better. I felt angry at Joyce and myself, forcing Dad to talk about his fear so that it wouldn't kill him. Everything seemed very real at this moment, and this thing was maybe thirty seconds away.

"David, what does this remind you of?" Joyce asked quickly. "What has been coming at you too fast, hunting you down?"

"My sickness!" Dad yelled. "Yes! That's what it is! That's how it feels! Like a shark swimming after me. Why me? What did I do to make this sickness come after me? It's so unfair! It's so — wait a minute, that's not a shark," he suddenly said. He leaned out of the boat to see. "It's something else. I know this from one of the books Phyllis gave me. It's not a shark, it's not as dangerous. What is it?"

I craned my neck to see if I could tell what it was, still alarmed at its speed. All I could see was that it was huge. Now that I looked, I could see it did not have a sharp fin like a shark's. But it wasn't a dolphin, it was . . .

"A WHALE!" Dad cried. The whale came close to the boat, then alongside of us, quickly swimming to get ahead of us. When it was many feet away, it sprang out of the water, flipped around to its other side, and splashed back into the ocean. "A whale! A whale! Just like in the books!" Dad was saying in his almost–eight-year-old voice. "It wasn't a shark, it was a beautiful whale!" I was speechless to see the ballerina grace of the spinning whale.

"David . . ." Joyce spoke softly.

"I know what it is!" Dad interrupted her. "You don't have to ask. I'll tell you what it is. It's not all bad! A shark might want to eat you for lunch, but a whale does not. My sickness is not out to get me. It's just my life, and life is full of beauty where you least expect it. It's not trying to hunt me down!" he said, starting to laugh. "Life is like a whale, because . . ." He was really trying to think this through. "Because, well, it's huge, it's bigger than I am, it seems a little too big to handle, and it's so beautiful, and full of . . . important things that are difficult to understand. How's that?" he asked.

Now Joyce was laughing. "I'd say you've done a lot of work, out there on the ocean! Do you think you're ready to come home now?"

Was it my imagination or was the boat starting to

speed up? Suddenly we were moving almost as fast as a motorboat toward something that was definitely not a tropical beach. This was the answer to Joyce's question. We were not homeward bound yet. There was something giant and white towering out of the ocean. I thought it might be a castle made of snow and reaching all the way up to the clouds, and I tried to guess what this could be. Maybe it was a pile of term papers that he had to grade, so huge they became the building blocks of an igloo castle. Maybe he'd been thinking he'd have to work twice as hard next year to make up for the time he'd lost. The boat came closer. This was something I'd only seen in pictures, never knowing how immense the real thing would be. It was an iceberg. An iceberg? Dad would have to start talking fast, or perhaps we would crash into it. But the boat slowed down and bobbed its way up to the side of this ice mountain whose top I could not even see.

"We've come to an iceberg," Dad said in a tired voice.

"Aha. I'm not surprised," Joyce said reassuringly. "Don't be discouraged, I'm sure we're close to the end of our journey, David. Let's just figure this out."

"I have no idea what this is," Dad said, shaking his head. "I'm afraid if I touch it, I'll freeze up, too. I'll turn to ice, and then into air."

I shivered when he said this, but not because I was cold.

"Touch it!" Out of nowhere, Joyce was insisting, "I have a strong feeling about this. Touch it now!"

The boat wobbled. She surprised me and Dad so much, we both jumped.

"Okay," Dad said cautiously, reaching out.

Silently, because he still hadn't seen me, I snuck to the edge of my seat and extended my arm, too.

The ice was not cold, but it sent some kind of feeling up my arm as quickly as fire or ice. What was it? I took a deep breath and realized that my mind was filling with memories coming one after another, faster than I thought my mind could think.

It was my first-grade teacher in an orange sweater out on the playground, telling us to look at the orange leaves of the fall trees. It was John telling all of us that we were going to "love love love" the black-and-white movie he found on channel thirteen, and all of us, my dad's friends and me, too full of Thanksgiving dinner to protest. It was Dad standing with me in the snow on a clear winter's night, pointing up at the sky and telling me the names of the constellations.

I looked over at Dad, his eyes closed as he touched the iceberg. When he spoke, his voice was absolutely clear. "I was afraid that if I didn't make it, if I actually died, my life would feel unfinished. But I can always look at it as a complete book, can't I? I mean, I can see all of you in it, and I am so grateful! And I will always be lucky for everything that has already happened. I've had so much fun, and I have loved my job, and you are the best friends I could ever want, and there's something on top of that, even more than that."

"What's that, David?" Joyce asked, but I could tell she was smiling as if she knew. What was it?

"Amalee," he said. "She is the most wonderful thing in my life. Her kindness to me, and her tomboy gracefulness that she doesn't even know she has, and her sense of humor." He opened his eyes. We were back in the room. "Amalee!" he said. "You're here!"

"I was here the whole time," I said. "I was here the whole time, Dad." I meant more than just our time in the boat today, and he knew it.

Dad said, "I'm sorry you had to go through all this, Honey."

"I was okay, Dad. I'm sorry you had to go through this. I wish you'd let me help you more. You could have told me you were frightened."

"I was obviously afraid of telling myself!" he said, laughing.

Joyce looked confused, and a little relieved. "Uh, three, two, one, now you're awake."

But he was already awake and we were all sitting on his bed together, no iceberg, no boat, and no more ocean.

I rested my head against Dad's chest, and he put his arm around me.

We sat quietly for a few minutes, and then we heard a car pull up outside. Soon Carolyn appeared in the doorway, and we all admired her painting.

Joyce marveled at the variety of plants Carolyn had painted, and I marveled at Joyce in a way I never had before.

Joyce said, "No wonder John's so excited about your work on the —" She stopped short.

"On what?" asked Dad.

"I'm, uh, helping John plant some stuff," Carolyn explained nervously. What was so hush-hush about that?

Joyce nodded her head, so whatever the secret was, she was in on it. She and Carolyn left the room and said they'd heat up some dinner for us.

I sat with Dad.

"Why couldn't you talk about being sick?" I asked.

"Why couldn't you tell me about school?" he asked.

"Hey, not fair," I said. "I was under strict orders from Dr. Nurstrom not to upset you."

"Well, I was under strict orders from the Patron Saint

of Parents not to tell my eleven-year-old daughter that I was so afraid of what was happening." So we both had a decent excuse.

"Do you want to tell me what happened at school?" he asked. "I know something happened."

"I don't want to, but I think I should." And so I started.

I started with Lenore asking me to stay over, then I told him about not having my notebooks, and finally I told him — slowly, exactly — what happened when I pushed Lenore and she fell down the stairs. I told him about how everybody hated me, and how Lenore was going to sue me and get me thrown out of school for a week, and that I thought I deserved it all until Phyllis stuck up for me. I ended by saying I still felt confused, and I still felt bad, but things were getting better.

"It turned into something like an English class," I said.

"What do you mean?" asked my dad.

"Well, I got to be the villain, and I survived. Ms. Severance says we need to understand the people we call the bad guys, and now I really do. So I feel lucky. And I also got to see that even when we do bad things, we can still be forgiven."

"So how does this terrible lesson make you lucky?"

my dad said, trying to make sense of this. "Oh, man. Honey, I feel like I really let you down."

"You let me down? I let you down! I'm the one who almost lost our house."

"No, that wouldn't have happened," Dad groaned. "I could have told you that. I could have helped you. I would have told you, well, first of all, you're not a villain or a bad guy. You're a great girl. I think you're the best. All my friends think you are the coolest kid."

"I haven't always been nice to your friends. I think sometimes I treated them like morons."

"Oh, big deal," he said. "Every once in a while you did what kids do. You said what was on your mind. They didn't care. I mean, they might have been hurt, but that's because they wanted you to like them. Adults pretend not to, but they really want kids to like them. When kids don't like you, you get afraid that you've forgotten what it's like to be a kid."

"Huh, I never thought of that."

"But my friends have always loved you. Right from the start. Every time I told them things you'd said or done, they were as proud as if they were your parents."

I thought of John putting my good tests on the refrigerator.

"Your friends are very interesting people," I said.

We both laughed a little. That was an understatement. I wasn't sure if I had taken them seriously before. I remembered thinking they were selfish, boring, weepy, whiny.

They were heroes! That's how I saw them now.

They were more than heroes. Each of them had a special skill that we needed to help my father.

"Your friends were superheroes," I said.

"Yeah," he said, shaking his head. "And I was the opposite."

"You were sick!" I protested. "Dad, you are still sick!"

"But I wonder how I could have come through for them if they were sick. Could I teach them philosophy?"

"No. You listen to them. If they were sick, you would sit and listen to them so much, your ears would get as big as satellite dishes."

"Oh, I see," he said.

"And your ears would transmit their messages across the planet, and thousands of people would send letters with helpful advice."

"Is that so?" Dad was laughing. "I don't think we should stop at this planet, then."

"You're absolutely right," I said. "Messages would be transmitted throughout the galaxy. And one very friendly extraterrestrial would show up, and he would say, 'JOYCE. WILL. YOU. BE. MY. GIRLFRIEND?'"

My dad laughed harder than he had in months. "I think Joyce is already taken, Honey," he said, wiping away his tears.

"Really?" I said. Well, good for Joyce.

"Or so I suspect," he added. I watched him look away mysteriously, and then he changed the subject. "Hey, what are they making us to eat in the kitchen?"

I got up and said I'd help them make some pesto and orecchiette. "*Orecchiette* just means pasta shaped like ears," I explained.

I stopped in the doorway and said, "Of course, you know you're already my hero."

My dad had already picked up his favorite gorilla book. He turned a little red.

"No, I didn't know that," he said, opening the pages.

"Oh, yeah. Your friends think I'm the coolest kid, but my friends think you're the coolest dad."

"You have friends?" he blurted out.

It was okay. He was allowed to wonder. I thought about it for a minute.

"I have one," I said.

CHAPTER SEVENTEEN

The Curtain Opens and the Stage Is Lit

I walked to school the next morning. Joyce had a boyfriend? Was it who I thought it was? I decided I'd ask her about it when I saw her again.

English class was great. Ms. Severance looked excited about the new words we were going to learn. She said, "These are words that you see all the time, but you might not know what they mean."

Ambivalent: having mixed feelings, feeling more than one way about something

Vigilant: watchful, often looking out for danger, making sure things go right

Pompous: having an exaggerated sense of self-importance, shown with boasting and grand gestures of seriousness

"How many of you have seen these words and wondered what they meant?" she asked.

We all raised our hands.

"Well, look them up!" Ms. Severance teased. "No, let's take the shortcut together. It's better to look at them here, because then we can talk about the sense of a word, or the connotation." She wrote "connotation" and underlined it. "Sentence?" she asked.

I raised my hand, and she called on me. "I was *ambivalent* about the advice from the expert, because I wanted to be *vigilant* about doing the right thing, but I knew he was so *pompous*, he might not be trustworthy."

I was speaking a secret language to Ms. Severance.

"Very good," she said cautiously. "Especially on the word 'pompous.'" She shot me a quick, knowing smile, then continued. "It's hard to trust pompous people, because they act like experts, but their own sense of self-importance can get in the way of their intelligence."

Poor Mr. Shapiro. If he only knew that I was having a conversation about him with Ms. Severance!

After class, I heard someone behind me in the hall.

"Hey, Amalee! Wait up!" It was Sarah. "We're doing three shows of *Bye Bye Birdie*. It's Thursday and Friday nights and Saturday afternoon. You want to come?"

"Sure!" I said. "How about Saturday afternoon?"

"Good," she answered. "We have the most tickets for that show." She pulled two tickets out of a big envelope and gave them to me.

Who would I invite? Lenore? Hally? Ellen? No, no, and no.

I decided to invite Phyllis. She loved to play tapes of Broadway musicals in her car. I bet she could sing along to the whole show.

But when I went to the office to invite her, Phyllis said she couldn't come, and she wouldn't say why.

"When does the play begin, and how long does it go?" she asked.

"It begins at two, and I guess it lasts two hours. Why?"

"Do you think you'll be home by six o'clock?" she asked secretively.

"Sure," I said.

Phyllis stopped looking so nervous. "Oh, good," she said. "Hey, is this the play your friend is in?"

"Sarah? Yeah."

"Why don't you invite her over afterward, for a little surprise?"

Surprise? Sarah? I wasn't sure I knew her well enough. "Oh, no, I couldn't do that," I said.

"Why not?" Phyllis laughed. "Oh, this is perfect. You and Sarah come home at six."

Hm. She was right. Why not?

I didn't let the problem of the two tickets bother me. I felt like Phyllis. I came up with a plan.

That night, I called Sarah and invited her over on Saturday. She answered the phone and said she'd love to come over, since the after-show party had been canceled.

She said, "This is great. I wanted to do *something* after a big performance."

"I'm sure your parents would take you out for ice cream," I said, curious to know if she had two parents at home.

"Oh, you'd be surprised," she said. "My parents can be *extremely* boring."

I heard a man and woman laughing in the background. "You hear that, Honey?" I heard a man say. "Don't mind us, Sarah. We're going to do something exciting, like go sit on the couch."

The woman laughed and so did Sarah.

"Actually, she's my stepmom," Sarah said. "Is Phyllis Francisco your stepmom?"

"Oh, no. She's my non-mom, but in a very important way."

"Ah, I get it," Sarah replied, and I could tell she did.

"Oh, speaking of which," I said, "there's no one who can come with me to the show, so I was wondering, do you need some help? Do you need an extra person to pin costumes or get anybody water or anything?"

Sarah checked the next day and slipped a note in my locker.

Guess who's going to a Bar Mitzvah on Saturday? Sammy. Guess what Sammy's job is? To pull the curtains! Come to the stage at one on Saturday, and they'll show you what to do.

Sincerely, Sarah

On Thursday, I left a bouquet of daffodils backstage, and I wrote a note saying, "Good luck!" And I also left an extremely huge piece of John's cake, which had still not run out.

On Saturday, I showed up a little before one.

The drama teacher, Ms. Bramson, wore a red skirt and a red sweater and had a red flower in her hair. She was brushing something off the end of her black feather boa. I think she'd dropped it in her caffe latte.

"I'm your curtain puller," I said.

"Excellent," she replied. "Excellent. Listen closely. When the lights go down, open the curtain." She opened her arms wide. She smelled like perfume and mothballs. "At the end of act one, when I signal, CLOSE the curtain." She closed her arms. "When the lights go down after intermission, OPEN the curtain, and when the show ends . . ."

I said, "CLOSE the curtain." I closed my arms.

"Yes, excellent! Oh, but then OPEN the curtain so they can take their bows. And if you don't do this perfectly, you'll never work in this town again!" She winked, kissed me on the top of my head, and with a whoosh turned and walked away, laughing.

And so I watched the whole show from the backstage, sitting on the same stool where I'd eaten lunch so many days. But now it was completely different.

The stage lights were on, and the stage glowed in purple, orange, and bright white. Eleven-, twelve-, and thirteen-year-olds were crowded backstage wearing lipstick. Some of them had white shoe polish in their hair to look older.

Ms. Bramson clutched a cup of coffee with her red fingernails as she stood on the other side of the stage, mouthing all the lines and even dancing some of the steps.

Sarah was truly the star. I was so excited that this nice, funny person was actually my friend. She even grabbed my hand and squeezed it before her first entrance.

"Wish me luck!" she'd whispered, heading out for her song.

I peeked down at the orchestra. For some reason, I felt very excited and choked up. Jimmy, the kid who had pretended to push me down the stairs, was playing the clarinet. He was sweating and nervous. He turned a page in his score, and it almost dropped off the music stand. He sweated some more.

He finished his part and looked up. Before I knew it, he'd caught my eye. I couldn't help it. I smiled and gave him a thumbs-up, and I wasn't kidding. The orchestra sounded good!

Before he could remember that he was about the meanest kid in school, he smiled back. And then he had to play again.

I couldn't wait to be involved in another play. Maybe I could help with costumes. I loved seeing these kids hunched over and nervous backstage, with coats over their shoulders. Suddenly one or two of them would throw off their coats and stride onto the stage, singing at the top of their lungs.

I felt like we had a little club backstage.

When the show was over, I helped Sarah get her costume packed up. She cleaned off her makeup, and then she hugged her friends. I talked a little bit with Marin, who had some great dance solos and a few lines to sing. We laughed about how nervous the kids in the orchestra were, especially Jimmy.

I said, "I felt bad for him."

"Oh, me, too!" she agreed.

Sarah came out and said to me and Marin, "My parents are going up to Woodstock next weekend, and they say there's a really cool candle store up there. You two want to come?"

I thought of the five of us in the car, laughing all the way up to Woodstock. It would be less crowded than a carload of my dad's friends! It seemed like a very, very good idea.

I got home with Sarah at around five-thirty. My dad was dressed in something other than sweatpants, and even had shoes on.

"Apparently, we're going out someplace," he said. "But no one will tell me where."

I introduced him to Sarah. I had to leave them alone for a few minutes, because I went into the bathroom, turned on the sink faucet, and started to cry.

I realized I never had thought I'd see my dad dressed up and ready to go out again. All those Friday nights I'd groaned through pizza and the movies with his friends, with him driving, humming along to the radio, and laughing at their jokes. Now all I wanted was that. I wanted to see my dad driving his car, humming and smiling, looking forward to the movie, looking forward to his job at the college, and looking forward to his life.

I took a few deep breaths. The first few were stuttery, but then they felt even. I splashed my eyes with water and went out to the living room.

"Sarah's stepmom and dad work at the college, too!" Dad said.

Joyce walked in, dressed in a beautiful purple silk dress, with a bright green scarf around her neck. "Is this your friend?" she asked, approaching Sarah.

"Yes," I said. "Joyce, this is Sarah."

Joyce hugged Sarah, and I hoped she wouldn't cry. She turned to my dad and spoke while Sarah recovered from her hug. "I'm the driver," she announced. "Right this way."

CHAPTER EIGHTEEN

The Secret's Out — Everyone Is Full of Surprises

Joyce cleared her junk from the seats in her car, laughing nervously as she picked up the gum wrappers, notebooks, and junk mail.

"I have a very . . . cluttered life, but an interesting one," she explained, doing a last arm brush of the seat for Sarah.

She tried to help Dad into the car, but he shook his head and slowly let himself in.

We drove toward town, with Joyce asking all sorts of questions. How was the play? How did we feel? Scared? Happy? We could have asked Joyce the same thing. She was all aflutter.

Dad was staring out at the town he hadn't seen for months. There were flowers around the mailboxes where he'd last seen snowbanks. Clearly, he didn't know where we were going, and he didn't care. But I did.

"Hey, I have a question," I butted in. "Where are we going?"

"To a restaurant," Joyce answered.

"The one where John works?" I asked.

"See for yourself. We're here." She stopped the car, and we all stared at the awning. It said, simply, JOHN AND FRIENDS. It was a restaurant. It was John's restaurant. It was John's restaurant that *belonged* to him! Under the awning was a big sign that said, GRAND OPENING!

"It can't be . . ." Dad began.

"I'm not going to cry," Joyce assured us, but her hands were shaking as she opened the door.

Silently, excitedly, we made our way into the building, which had been boarded up for a while. But not anymore. It was crowded! Crowded with people, plants, candles, and walls painted with vines.

The first thing we saw, though, was a simple waiting area, next to the coatroom, with a light-blue tiled floor, white walls, and a light-gray stone fountain — just a stone bowl on a small pillar, with water spouting in three silver sprays.

"Do you like it?" Joyce asked. "I put it together. I worked with someone at Carolyn's gardening store."

"It's really nice, Joyce," Sarah spoke up.

"You see, Sarah, this is a little embarrassing, but whenever I see something beautiful, I want to cry. There's nothing wrong with it, except sometimes I realize I think I *have* to cry or else nobody in the room will feel anything. So the fountain is there to remind me that I don't have to do all the crying, as it were," Joyce explained in a rush of words. "Everyone's a fountain, right?" She gave me and Dad a knowing look.

"Yes, everyone has the right to be lachrymose," I noted. They all looked at me.

"Well, while John was secretly opening this place, I was secretly learning new words in school!" I exclaimed, and then I looked at the fountain and said, "I love it, Joyce. You are very talented!"

"You think *I'm* talented." She laughed. "Hey, Phyllis, come be our tour guide!"

Phyllis appeared at a small podium in the corner. She was wearing a long black dress. Her hair was swooped up in a silver clip, and she was wearing a long silver necklace.

"Look at you!" Dad exclaimed.

"No, David," she protested, "look at *you*!" Then she cleared her throat and said, "Come right this way, everyone."

I saw how the painted vines climbed up and wound their way all around the bottom half of the walls. Very dramatic.

I looked over as a camera flashed. The local paper was taking a picture of Carolyn signing her masterpiece in a corner under a bunch of grapes. So this was the project she had been doing with John!

Sarah and I swung around as we heard another sound. John himself came bursting through the doors that swung out from the kitchen. "Goodness! Look at the crowd!" he exclaimed, addressing us as if he were an emperor in a chef's hat.

"I put ads in all the papers and on the radio," Phyllis whispered to us. "The ads said, 'Come to our new restaurant, and for five dollars you can try everything on the menu.' Cheap food and a chance to sample everything. It seemed like good marketing."

So Phyllis had organized this whole thing. I hadn't even thought to notice all the files, folders, and envelopes she had added to her usual pile. She was always busy working on a few ideas. Now the plan was to make a big splash with the opening for John's restaurant, and she had obviously succeeded!

"If I can make parents' night sound like fun, why not

a new restaurant?" she added modestly, but I could tell she was very proud.

I saw that the menu had been blown up to poster size, standing on an easel, and I realized all of the dishes were being served in miniature on trays that were being passed around.

John was being very good at being John, making his way through the crowd, saying things like, "You're sure? You are positively sure the pie crust is flaky and delicious?" and "Well, I could give you the recipe, but then I'd have to kill you," and "Well, if you love it, then have another one!"

"That's John," I said, pointing him out to Sarah. She was eating a little spinach quiche. "Uh-oh. John said we wouldn't like that until we were fourteen," I warned her.

"I like it now!" she said with her mouth full, picking another one off the tray. "Can we call my dad and stepmom?"

"Sure!" I said, and Phyllis appeared out of thin air with a phone. Sarah disappeared to call her house.

Everyone was gaping at the beautiful walls.

I snuck up next to Carolyn and said, "That's some *trompe l'oeil*."

Carolyn put her arm around me, bony but strong. Her

red hair was extra spiky tonight. Very fancy. "Thank you," she said. "I know. But what about the plants? The living ones. Do they look healthy? I raised them myself."

I looked around at the potted trees and the planters on the low walls.

"Hm . . ." I said. Carolyn watched me nervously. "I'd say they look so good, people will come here just for the beauty of the place."

Carolyn exhaled. "I thought so myself, but I didn't want to say it. I'm very modest. Hey, look at that dessert table!"

Sarah had returned, and she and I looked over at a long table covered with desserts. Cakes, custards, linzer torte . . . everything John and I had made in the kitchen that night and more.

Carolyn had handwritten the labels: BROOKLYN BLACK-OUT CAKE, WOODSTOCK CARROT CAKE, HUDSON RIVER BLUE-BERRY PIE, SAVANNAH LEMON MERINGUE PIE, and, of course, RASPBERRY LINZER TORTE.

"Amalee, look," said Carolyn, nodding toward the door. Dr. Nurstrom walked in. I saw him laugh as he shook my dad's hand. I was glad to see that Dad was sitting. Joyce had been standing close by — protecting him, I think. Dad looked happy. Dr. Nurstrom looked happy. He put his arm around Joyce.

"Dr. Nurstrom is dating Joyce," Carolyn said. "Didn't you notice?"

"I only knew about the one date!" I said. Carolyn didn't have a chance to answer.

"Hey!" came a voice from behind me. "How is my little girl?"

I turned around and saw John. His voice did not match the look on his face. He looked almost bashful, as if he were waiting for my approval.

I remembered what Dad said, about adults wanting kids to like them.

I decided to come clean, right then and there. "John, when I said you'd never open a restaurant I felt terrible! I felt terrible for days! I felt like a jerk. And I'm so glad I was wrong."

"Oh, Honey, I have to thank you for that!" John assured me cheerfully. "I was so freaked out when you said that, I thought, *Have I really been saying this over and over?* I decided to get the God's honest truth about it, so guess who I called?"

"Carolyn?" I guessed.

"That's right," he said. "She said whenever I started talking about my job, she felt like she was stuck on an elevator with bad music from her prom."

He went on to explain that after our night in the

kitchen, he'd marched himself into the bank, gotten a loan approved, and made an offer on this very building that afternoon.

"Even after that Friday night when I cursed you by opening my big mouth?" I asked.

"Big and beautiful, Sweetheart, and don't you go changing!"

I found out that when John bought the building, all his friends jumped in to help. Carolyn painted the inside and some of the outside, designed the menus, and printed all the signs. After painting all those incredibly detailed, beautiful plants, she decided she wanted to grow real plants, and to grow some for the restaurant.

Joyce, as it turned out, didn't just build the fountain. She had helped Carolyn paint and had picked out the tables and chairs. She also insisted on buying some fancy kitchen things for John, like a giant stove! She said she'd been saving up money for a rainy day, and one stormy Tuesday she decided *this rainy day is as good as any*.

Phyllis had not only planned this opening night. She had also hired the waitstaff, created a schedule for them, and made contacts with all the local farmers so that John could work with them. She was going to work at the restaurant at night, taking care of all the money issues, making sure that everything was "in the black," as she put it.

For his part, John had been dreaming about his restaurant for so long, he merely had to walk in, crack an egg, and start cooking, just like he had at our house.

Phyllis snuck up behind me and put a hand on my shoulder.

"Not bad for a bunch of misfits, huh?"

I felt my body get tense. She knew that's how *I* had seen them. Suddenly I was right back there on a Friday night, rolling my eyes in my dad's small car, waiting for his friends to do something, anything, about their problems. And Phyllis knew that's how I'd felt.

But then I looked up and saw her face. She was beaming with pride. "Isn't this beautiful?" she asked.

We both looked all the way around the restaurant, at John smiling and eating his own tiny quiches, Carolyn showing a detail of her painting to my art teacher, Joyce laughing, Dr. Nurstrom smiling, Dad picking out a shrimp dumpling from a tray, and all the other people who had shown up tonight, thanks to Phyllis.

"You aren't misfits," I mumbled, completely embarrassed.

"Oh, yeah? Well, guess what?" Phyllis asked. "Neither are you. By the way, those girls I saw you with at the beginning of the year, what were their names again?"

"Hally and Ellen?"

"Hally and Ellen, that's it. I could tell you felt uncomfortable around them."

"They like to make fun of people." I was finally understanding how unhappy I had felt, trying to win their favor.

I thought Phyllis didn't hear me. "I always felt bad for them," she said. Really? "They'll never learn about their own lives if they keep on criticizing the way other people walk and talk and dress." She paused and thought and said, "Ugh. I think I was like them when I was your age."

REALLY?

"We all want to impress people, you know," she went on. "And when we find people we don't have to impress, you know what we call them? We call them friends."

I thought of John telling his friends, including my dad, that he felt like a depressed cow. What a field day Hally and Ellen would have with that!

"And you know what the truly magical thing is?" Phyllis continued. "A real friendship doesn't ask you to impress anyone, and yet it helps you do all sorts of impressive things you never thought you could do!"

Then Phyllis sounded a little like a teacher as she

asked, "And what do you think is the key to that magic door?"

"I don't know, Phyllis," I said. "I'm not so good at finding this magic door yet. I'm a work in progress on this topic."

She countered, "Well, why do you think you invited Sarah here tonight?"

I thought of the day I met Sarah. We probably hit it off because I didn't make her feel like a "misfit," as Phyllis would say, for wandering around backstage, and she didn't make fun of me for eating lunch alone in the dark. That's when we knew we could be friends.

I looked over at Sarah now, talking with John. She must have said something nice about his cooking, because suddenly he was hugging her in his enormous way. I was relieved to see she didn't give him a you're-so-weird look. She just laughed.

I turned to Phyllis and said, "I know the answer. If the door you're talking about is friendship, there is no key. If you want to open the magic door, you have to knock, and you have to keep knocking until someone opens it up from the other side. Right? Is that what you were thinking?"

Phyllis beamed. "Bright, bright, bright as a star. I love the way that mind of yours works, Amalee Everly." I guess it was better than the answer she was looking for. I took that as a good sign.

Across the room, Dad held something up. It looked like a dumpling, "Have you had one of these?" he called. "It's amazing! You have to try it!"

I made my way across the room to where Dad was sitting with Joyce and Dr. Nurstrom. "I will!" I answered.

Tonight, I would try anything.